99

3

39
9
9

0

WITHDRAWN

Death sounds grand

At the time of his violent death, Professor Robert Higgins, a brilliant and wealthy Cambridge physicist, was privately using his knowledge of those sounds known to penetrate the human subconscious to create a device that would calm disturbed minds – en masse. Then the dangers of football riots and picket-line violence could be a thing of the past. At short range, though, he found that his prototype was an extremely dangerous weapon, one that was the subject of intense interest, and not only to a certain government department...

So, when a series of minor robberies appeared to have been accomplished with the help of this stolen 'hypnotizer', Detective Chief Inspector Sidney Walsh and his attractive Constable, Brenda Phipps, knew they were on the scent of a ruthless and dangerous quarry.

The alibi of the dead professor's widow was as shaky as the avarice of her son was suspicious, whilst the beautiful hypnotist, Marion Dubonnet, came highest on the list of beneficiaries in Higgins's will. But the sudden deaths of two of the latter's laboratory colleagues followed swiftly, and when the life of Inspector Walsh himself was also threatened, the killer's nerve seemed stretched to breaking point.

Richard Hunt's second crime novel is an ingenious cat's cradle of anarchy, dissimulation and madness.

Also by Richard Hunt

Death in ruins (1991)

DEATH
SOUNDS GRAND

Richard Hunt

Constable · London

First published in Great Britan 1991
by Constable & Company Ltd
3 The Lanchesters, 162 Fulham Palace Road
London W6 9ER
Copyright © 1991 Richard Patrick Hunt
ISBN 0 09 470680 8
The right of Richard Patrick Hunt to be
identified as the author of this work has been
asserted by him in accordance with the
Copyright, Designs and Patents Act 1988
Set in Linotron Palatino and
printed in Great Britain by
Redwood Press Limited
Melksham, Wiltshire

A CIP catalogue record for this book
is available from the British Library

1

The Cambridge sky was heavily overcast, making the late evening light into the darkness of early night.

Only a few people strolled the intersecting footpaths of the meadowland that spread from the Trumpington Road down to the river and beyond, but some of those that did gave a nod or grunt of recognition to the familiar, tall, gangly, grey-haired man in the loose-fitting black suit. Or perhaps those nods and grunts were for the aged, overweight golden retriever that plodded gamely along beside him. In fact there was probably more chance that the dog would return the greeting than the man, for Professor Higgins was deep in serious thought, as usual.

This evening, though, his mask of concentration was broken by the faintest of smiles, creasing the corners of his mouth.

The recollection of his conversation with his colleague Professor Hughes, some months previously, was amusing him. They'd been discussing the inability of the college's Benevolent Trust fund to meet all this year's demands on it, genuine though each case was. It would not have been a problem, had there not been a rule preventing the trustees from making personal contributions. Higgins would gladly have made up the shortfall himself, from his own resources. Then Professor Hughes had suggested that a sizeable *ex gratia* donation might be available if he were prepared to develop some of his published theories. He hadn't really liked the idea of dealing with a government department in secret, but the amount of money was considerable and would solve the fund's problems for this year, and next year as well, probably.

So he had agreed.

What was really so amusing was that the development had gone so well. His theories had been vindicated: the prototype he had built successfully demonstrated that. Mind you, in hindsight, he had made some rather bold claims; success wouldn't have been possible without the use of the very latest computer-linked techniques.

So he'd proved himself right, and thoroughly enjoyed himself while doing so. There were still a lot of problems to overcome before the project was complete, though.

He shook his head violently, as though to stir his brain cells into greater activity, causing some concern about his mental stability in a bewildered lady passing the other way with a yappy, white terrier.

Problems were the spice of life to an active brain like his. There was bound to be a way; it just required concentration and thought. There were several logical lines for further development. He'd do some work on his computer model when he got home; Madge, his wife, had gone out, to some party or other, so there need be no distractions.

He turned from the river path near a narrow wooden bridge, where several punts were moored beneath the hanging tresses of willows that leaned far out over the murky water. Sheba, the golden retriever, undertook her nightly duty of disturbing the wary ducks from the river bank. Their protesting squawks seemed adequate compensation for the effort involved.

Professor Higgins headed back homewards.

Whichever way the final problems were resolved, it would mean a vastly more complex and unwieldy apparatus than the neat, portable piece of equipment that he had already constructed, and many computer program amendments.

He felt quite pleased with himself as his feet crunched into the gravel of his own driveway. It had become quite dark now. The shrubs and bushes were only vague shapes against the blacker background of the hedges and trees.

He paused in surprise as he noticed the glow of a light from one of the windows on the side of the house.

'I've left the light on in the study again,' he said out loud, shrugging his shoulders philosophically. It was a problem, having to remember to do the petty things in life, like leaving the front door catch up so that it didn't matter if he'd forgotten his keys. He opened the front door and released the catch; Madge mustn't find it like that when she got home from wherever she had gone. It might lead to another episode of shouted words and argument, and he didn't want that. He walked through the hallway and opened the door to his study. He was confused, because the room was in darkness except for the eerie green glow from the computer screen.

'I must have imagined it,' he muttered to himself as he switched the main light on and strode over to the table by the wall. Then he looked down in even greater bewilderment at the screen, which displayed the flickering words 'Copying Program'. That was a current instruction, still being performed. It couldn't have been left on all night.

A hooded figure slipped out from the darkness behind the door and tiptoed cautiously behind the Professor as he leaned forward to stare at the little red light of the whirring, copying tape streamer. The figure swung a short length of lead piping, viciously, and hit the back of Robert Higgins's head with a crunching blow, then, to be on the safe side, hit him again as he crumpled to his knees.

The intruder let out a snarl of irritation at this interruption of well-made plans and angrily kicked the motionless body before bending down to feel for a pulse at the neck of

7

the unconscious man. There was a slight flicker of movement under the finger.

The figure stood up and looked round. The tape had finished copying. It was put in a Sainsbury's carrier bag, together with the lead pipe and a small black box on which had been written the words 'Prototype One' in large white letters.

The dark figure switched off the light and went through the hallway, passed the sleepy Sheba and left by the front door, pulling it to so that the Yale lock clicked loudly in the silence of the night. The black cotton hood was removed and a bicycle was dragged out from behind a shrub. Then the figure mounted and rode off down the avenue to the main road, keeping close into the darkness of the hedges; then it pedalled furiously towards the town.

Twenty minutes later Robert Higgins suffered a second haemorrhage, and passed quietly out of this world into one in which, presumably, there would be no problems for him to solve.

The four single headlights wound their way carefully down the rough winding track, into the small copse. The engines throbbed gently, but there was a confidence about the riders that suggested it wasn't the first time they had made the journey.

Once they were safely in the small clearing at the centre, however, the engines roared exhilaratingly and the motor cycles raced round in perilous confusion, weaving and crossing each other's paths, the riders shouting and yelling riotously, to emphasize their individual skills.

Eventually, though, they swung round in a circle, turned in at the four corners of a square and stopped, so that their dipped headlights illuminated the flat, grassy area.

The roar of the engines died away and the rustling of the dying autumn leaves again predominated.

The burly, well-built group leader, resplendent in studded and badged black gear, took off his helmet and unzipped the front of his jacket.

'Come on then, girl. If you want to join our group you know what you've got to do now,' he grunted, as he pulled at the ring of a can of lager and tipped his head back to drink.

The slim, brown-leather-clad figure behind him slid off the back of the bike and stood, hesitantly, as though having second thoughts about going through with the ritual initiation ceremony of this particular group of so-called Hell's Angels.

'Git on with it,' came a slurred voice from one of the other bikes.

The girl steeled herself and stepped into the lighted area, reaching up to take her helmet off and shaking free her dark hair. Once started she seemed to gain confidence: the leather jacket came off next, then the heavy boots and the over-trousers, the T-shirt, jeans and skimpy cotton undergarments. Divested of clothes, she seemed even more slender and fragile. A lovely, firm, mature white body.

Fully committed now, she showed bravado, pirouetting round in the glare of the lights, raising her arms above her head and jerking her hips from side to side, seductively, like some South Sea Island hula girl. Then she stood still, legs apart and hands on hips, waiting.

The burly boy tossed the empty can to one side and strolled casually behind her, reaching to take her firm full breasts in his hands. For some moments he worked the supple flesh in his fingers and palms, then he ran a hand slowly down, over the smooth stomach, into the mass of curly hair.

'You go first, George, she's a bit tight for me, yet,' he called, pushing the girl towards one of the other bikes. She walked away, loose-limbed and free, and then stopped, hesitated, staring forward with narrowed eyes into the darkness beyond the lights. Her hand came up, a finger pointing forward.

'There's someone by that tree, watching us,' she cried out, her voice pitched high in nervous excitement.

The burly boy glanced in the direction of her finger, then leapt on his bike, pushing it off the stand and kicking at the starter all in one movement.

'Get the bastard,' he yelled, before the roar of the engine drowned his voice.

As he swung the bike across the grass the naked girl leapt for the pillion, grabbing the boy's shoulder. The lights revealed a dark figure, jigging, running through the bushes. With a whoop the burly boy kicked up a gear and roared in pursuit, into the undergrowth. The front wheel hit a stump at an angle, veering the bike into a tree. The girl somersaulted twice, landed on her back and lay very still, arms outstretched, helplessly exposed and utterly desirable, except for the blood welling from the inside of her white thigh where a broken branch had impaled her.

Still pretty in her late forties, slim and elegant in a new long, Indian cotton dress, her fair hair brushed neatly in a casual early Lady Di style, Madge Higgins arrived at the reception, earlier than usual, and was a little surprised at the number of guests already there. Fortunately, she'd found a convenient place to park her car, just a little way down the road from the big house, near a small side gate from which she thought she might be able to make her exit without attracting attention later on.

She was welcomed by Councillor Stevens and his wife in the hallway. Stevens put a familiar arm round Madge's shoulders, and drew her into one of the downstairs rooms to introduce her to some Australian guests.

Madge took a glass of wine from a passing tray, at the same time managing to escape the embarrassing encircling

10

arm, and chatted sociably. She soon grew bored with talk of distant trade unions, although much too polite to show it, and took the first opportunity that occurred to escape. She wanted to circulate among the guests and be seen by as many people as she could, in the shortest possible time.

Her experience of such events stood her in good stead. It enabled her to work her way from group to group in the various rooms, greeting people effusively and generally acting out the part of the lone woman bent on an evening's socializing.

There were several people that she did not know. A grey-suited, tubby, middle-aged man had sat down alone in a corner with a drink in his hand, with the intention, presumably, of studying the others in the room. She felt his eyes watching her and was happy to pass on, out of that room. Eventually she stole a glance at her watch then slipped, unobtrusively, out of a side door, made her way down the narrow path to the small gate, and drove hurriedly away.

'It's all right, Sheila. I know all about the others on the motor bikes and what was going on, but that's no concern of ours,' Detective Constable Brenda Phipps said at the hospital bedside.

The girl's dark hair contrasted with her face, which was nearly as pale as the pillow.

'What the hell do you want then?' she asked resentfully.

'The man you saw in the bushes. Can you describe him?'

'Don't know if it was a man, I couldn't tell in the dark, could I? But I suppose it was. He was dressed in dark clothes. I think he was peering through something, or seemed to be, like a box it was, a black box, I saw it better when he turned to run, it hung round his neck on a string. A camera, I suppose it could have been.'

11

2

Six feet tall, broad-shouldered and grey-suited, Sidney James Walsh, Detective Chief Inspector with the Cambridgeshire Constabulary, stood looking down at the body of Professor Robert Higgins, wondering how many such sights he had witnessed during his career. He raised his greying but still handsome head, and looked thoughtfully round the room.

On a solid-looking table there was a small computer unit with a matrix printer, fed from a box of continuous stationery. Under the window stood a large oak, double pedestal desk, littered with papers and journals. It was a light and airy room, with wide windows and pretty chintz curtains. Along the short wall were shelves full of technical and reference books. The only other large item of furniture was an old leather armchair with a soft feather-filled cushion on which brightly coloured roses were embroidered.

The room was full of specialists from the Scene-of-Crime team. The police doctor, in a light grey suit, and Richard Packstone, the tall, bespectacled head of the forensic department, knelt by the body. Another man dusted white powder on to the computer keyboard, and a photographer held up his camera. Walsh failed to turn his head quickly enough to avoid the blinding light of the flash. He blinked a few times to help his eyes recover. Someone else was on all fours, studying the carpet intently.

By the door, also just watching, stood the slim figure of Detective Constable Brenda Phipps, dressed in eye-catching tight blue jeans and a leather jacket. A lock of brown hair fell forward over her angelic oval face, and was flicked away with a slender brown hand.

She smiled and shrugged her shoulders when she saw Walsh looking at her. Their time would come when all the experts had done their surface scanning, and taken their photos and minute dust samples.

The doctor and Packstone heaved themselves upright from beside the body.

'The time of death was probably between eight and eleven o'clock last night, Sidney,' the doctor said, slipping his folded spectacles into his top pocket. 'The autopsy will be more specific, but that is something for you to go on for the time being. The cause of death is heavily inflicted blows to the left lower back of the cranium, resulting in a depressed fracture. Pretty hard hits to achieve that. Those are the only injuries we can detect at this stage. If death did not occur instantaneously, then the pressure caused by the internal bleeding would almost certainly have led to a fatality within a very short period. You can move the body now, if you wish.'

'Are you finished with the body, Smith?' Walsh called out to the photographer who was now studying the light switch.

'Yes, thanks,' came the reply.

'Brenda, ask the ambulance men to take him away, please,' Walsh asked quietly.

'To fall just how he did, he was probably leaning forward over the table when the first blow was made,' Richard Packstone suggested. 'Bearing that in mind, to make an estimate of the killer's height is difficult, but I'd say he was on the shorter side of average.'

The doctor looked thoughtful. 'I'm inclined to agree, but

it'd be unwise to rely on that too much; far too many unknown factors.'

'Average height? Male or female?' Walsh asked.

Packstone shrugged his shoulders. 'We might find something to indicate sex when we've done all our tests on surface traces and dust from that area behind the door, where the killer probably stood when Higgins came back, but I wouldn't bank on that.'

Packstone turned away to give some instructions to one of his Scene-of-Crime assistants, and the doctor waved a jaunty hand as he left.

'Come on, Brenda, let's look round outside while this lot get finished,' Walsh said, not impressed by the information gleaned from that conversation.

They went through the french windows in the dining-room on to a sunlit, paved terrace that ran along the back of the house. Before them stretched a long, closely mown lawn with edges scalloped round rose beds and shrubberies. The gentle breeze stirred the leaves on the tall trees that bordered the grounds, a whispering accompaniment to the virtuoso performances of dozens of birds.

Walsh took this all in with a single glance, then concentrated his attention on the downstairs windows and doors as they walked round the house. The paint on the kitchen door had several scratches near the bottom, but none were fresh or near the lock.

'They've got a dog,' volunteered Brenda, helpfully. Walsh nodded and moved on, but they found no signs of forced entry.

On the wide gravelled driveway he stood for several moments with his hands in his pockets, looking up at the imposing frontage of the large Victorian house.

'It's funny they can't find anything missing, isn't it? There's plenty of good stuff in there that a thief would be glad to get his hands on.' He shrugged his shoulders phlegmatically. 'We'll have to assume that entry was made through a door that was already unlocked unless the killer had his own key,' he muttered, half to himself, 'but there's no way out of the grounds at the back, so he must have left this way.'

To Brenda, the surface of the gravel on the drive, which swept round from one entrance in the tall hedge bordering the road, across the front of the house, then out again further down, conveyed nothing, but Walsh followed its length, studying it intently. Occasionally he bent his knees and inclined his head near the ground, then crossed to the other side, and repeated the process. Eventually he stood up, brushing the knees of his suit, and strode purposefully over to the laurel hedge.

'Bike,' he said positively, pointing to some marks in the dry soil and then to a few stems in the bushes that were unnaturally bent and out of place.

'Could be the paper boy, Chief,' Brenda suggested.

Walsh shook his head. 'I don't think so. He seems to come in the other entrance, and doesn't get off his bike. He can reach the letter box without, same with the postman.'

'Wouldn't Higgins have seen a bike there, when he came back from walking his dog?'

'No reason why he should, Brenda, he'd have used the other entrance. Still, someone pushed a bike in the hedge here recently. You can just make out the wheel tracks where they cross the ridges in the gravel, just there, see. Ask Packstone to give this bit a going over. You can make a note to have a word with the newspaper boy and the postman to confirm what I think, and we'd better find out about any bikes stolen last night, just in case one of them was used.'

Packstone looked impressed at the story Walsh had gleaned from the surface of the drive.

15

'I'll get my boys on to it, Sidney, it all helps,' he said over his shoulder, as he hurried back into the house.

'We'll need to find out if he was expecting any visitors, and whether the neighbours saw anyone,' Walsh remarked, tapping his hand thoughtfully. 'Also that computer in there, Brenda. Either Higgins or the killer may have been using it, so we'll need to know what the programs are about. Get in touch with our computer expert chappie and see what he can make of it, then find out whether Mrs Higgins has recovered enough for us to talk to her.'

The lounge was a bright, spacious room with high ceiling, moulded plaster covings and rich furnishings. One or other of the Higginses had good taste.

'Good afternoon, Mrs Higgins, I'm Sidney Walsh, Detective Chief Inspector, and this is Detective Constable Phipps. I'm so very sorry about your husband. Are you sure you feel well enough to talk to us?' Walsh asked, as he walked over to where she was sitting.

She was wearing a grey dress with faint white vertical stripes that made her look taller than she probably was. Her hair was brushed neatly back from her forehead, and the skin of her face was softly smooth, but very pale.

'I remember meeting you and your wife at one of our charity functions, Inspector. Of course I'm ready to answer any questions you need to ask, but this has been a terrible shock to me, as you can imagine. Do sit down, both of you,' she replied bravely, in a soft, well-modulated voice. 'Now, how can I help? I must warn you that when it comes to my husband's work, I won't be able to tell you very much.'

'That doesn't matter, just tell me a bit about him.'

'He was a brilliant intellectual, even when I first met him. I suppose that was what attracted me to him, his air of self-confidence. I was in my early twenties when I married

16

him, you see. I only learned later that he was a very insular and introverted man, with next to no social graces. So intent on his own thoughts he didn't have the patience to talk about matters of general interest. He had his hobbies, of course, but even then he couldn't do something simple. Animal communication sounds fascinated him, and he took that just as seriously as he did his physics. I'm much more of an artistic person, so we didn't have a lot in common.'

Something in the tone of her voice suggested to Walsh that she'd used those same words many times before. Her social chat lines, presenting herself as a misunderstood woman, perhaps.

'Any children?' he asked.

'Just one son, Inspector. John's married now and runs his own business in Royston. Doing very well, I believe.'

'Was your husband expecting any visitors last night, do you know?'

'He didn't tell me if he was, Inspector, but it's unlikely. His friends, if you can call them that, were all college people. Most of the people that come here are my friends. He'd usually go off, then, to his study, to be on his own.'

'Did he have any enemies, or anyone who might have wanted him out of the way, for any reason?' Walsh asked, watching her closely. Her face was a little flushed now, and she leaned back on the settee, the fingers of her left hand lightly rubbing her cheek. Was she acting out a part? There was not very much outward show of grief at the death of her husband. Surely, emotion and tears would have been the first choice for an actress, unless she was convinced that such a part would not be tenable in the long run. Something wasn't quite right.

'The answer to your question isn't straightforward. I know of no one who could be considered an enemy in a physical sense, but there are several individuals who might be considered his rivals for prestige, or even possibly honours. People who would be keen to find out his latest developments in physics theories. He was quite often well in advance of his contemporaries, you see,' she replied with a slight smile.

'And the names of these people?' Walsh asked.

'I think it would be far better if you obtained a list from his colleagues at college. He used to mumble a few names to me sometimes, but to be honest, I never took much notice,' she admitted.

'Your husband was a physicist, then?'

'Yes, he lectured at Downing College, but he was also occasionally involved in research. His current project was to do with his hobby, sound and animal behaviour, he worked on that here at home.' Mrs Higgins ran her hand over her temples.

'He used the computer in his study for that, did he?'

'Yes, I suppose so, I'm not really sure. I didn't go in there very often. That room was his private place, and I wasn't welcome.'

'I gather that you weren't at home yesterday evening, Mrs Higgins. Would you mind telling me where you went, and what time you got back?'

Mrs Higgins licked her lips and her eyes looked towards the window. 'I went to a party at Councillor Stevens' house. It was on behalf of a charity for orphaned Sudanese children, if I remember correctly. I didn't get home until the early hours of this morning. Everything here appeared to be perfectly normal. I didn't see Robert, we have separate bedrooms, you understand. I assumed that he was in bed and asleep.' Her voice tailed off and the colour had completely left her face. 'Inspector, I'm sorry, but I'm not feeling very well now. I think I'd better go and lie down. Perhaps I'll take one of the tablets the doctor left me. Would you mind very much if we continued this conversation some other time?'

She pushed herself up from the settee, tottering slightly.

18

There were many more questions that Walsh needed to ask, but there was no hurry, tomorrow would do just as well. He stood up. 'Of course, it's perfectly understandable. I'll ring you in the morning and we'll see how you are then.' He watched thoughtfully as Mrs Higgins left the room.

'Well, my dear, I must say I don't think you look old enough to be a policewoman, and a detective one, at that. How exciting! I suppose you must be one of these career women you read about, and you so pretty too. Still, you've got plenty of time to get married and have a family.' Old Mrs Palgrave was chatting while she poured out the tea.

'It's about your neighbour across the road, Mrs Palgrave. Professor Higgins,' Brenda Phipps added, carefully taking the bone china teacup from an aged and shaky hand.

'Oh yes! Poor Robert Higgins, I could hardly believe it when Nurse Thompson told me about it this morning. She comes in every day, to make sure I've taken those nasty pills the doctor insists I have. They don't do any good, but he won't listen. Yes, poor Robert, I mean, I saw him last evening, when he came back from his walk with the dog, striding along, hale and hearty, full of life, and now he's passed on. You never can tell, can you?'

'You actually saw him come back last night, Mrs Palgrave? But you can't see the road from this room, because of the hedge.'

'Oh no, my dear, I was in my bedroom, upstairs. I go to bed early these days, mind you. I've got a television up there, if there's anything I want to watch, which isn't very often, I'm afraid. Don't they put on some awful programmes these days? How on earth they think they can justify the licence fee, I'll never know.'

'How long were you watching? Out of the window, I

19

mean. Can you remember seeing anyone else shortly afterwards? Someone on a bicycle, perhaps?'

'Oh dear me! You know, I don't think I can. You see, I often drop off to sleep in my chair by the window. Sometimes I spend the whole night there, well wrapped up, of course, even though I'm next to the radiator.'

'How far down the avenue can you see? As far as the main road?' Brenda asked.

The old lady patted her silver hair with one hand and reached for her stick with the other. 'You'd best come up and see for yourself,' she replied.

Brenda moved the white net curtains in the bedroom's bay window.

'You see? Sitting here, I've got a good view down the road, haven't I? At night I can see the lights when a car turns off the Trumpington Road. I remember Madge Higgins's car coming home last night, too. It was much later than usual for her. Quarter to three. I know that, my dear, because the grandfather clock in the hall chimes the quarters. Lovely old clock that, you won't see many finer. It was my Great Aunt Jane's, you know, you must have a look at it when we go downstairs.'

3

'He was a lovely man, the poor Professor was, Inspector,'
Mrs Byatt said, dabbing at her eyes with a man-sized handkerchief. 'Ten years or so I've worked for him, and a real
gentleman he was, never too proud but he'd have time for a
word and a laugh with his daily help, if you know what I
mean, leastways most of the time, 'cos sometimes when he
was thinking, he'd not even know you was there, like. But
you couldn't blame him for that, could you? Him being a
professor and all. Mind you, I can't say I'd have liked to
have been married to him. He didn't watch the telly or go
down the pub like a real man would, but he was happy in
his own way. Live and let live, I say. He got on the missus's
wick at times, though. They've had their rows over the
years, particularly about that son of theirs, but he weren't
much of a husband for her, I will say that. She'd doll herself
up, pretty like, but it didn't seem to get him worked up, if
you know what I mean, well, not to my knowledge,
anyway. They've had separate bedrooms ever since I've
known them. Grass widow, that's what she was. Mind
you, she's a selfish bitch too, in her own way, although I
shouldn't say it really, and she's lonely, for all her society
friends and parties and that sort of thing. Spoilt as a girl, I
always thought.' She folded her plump arms into her lap.

'You say they had words about their son. Why was that?'
Walsh inquired.

'I never did like him, that boy of theirs, nor that girl he got hitched up to. Nasty piece of work, to my mind. It was about money. He always thought he could touch his dad whenever he felt like it, but there came a time when the Professor had had enough, and said, "No more." Quite right too, and not before time, but it upset his missus. Me, I've been ever so lucky with my lad, he's growing up a lovely chap, and he's doing well for himelf. He works down at the computer shop in town. He understands all that sort of stuff, micro bits and VDU things, even though what they mostly sell is videos and cassettes. Where he gets the brains from, I don't know, but I'd do anything for my lad. Give her credit, Mrs Higgins dug into her own pocket for her boy, silly fool. Mind you, neither of them are short of a bob or two, but don't think the Professor was a miser, oh no, he'd help someone if he thought they deserved it. Often I've heard her tell him he was a soft touch for a sob story, but I've always been gone home by four o'clock, so I can't tell you anything about their evening visitors. It ain't half a shame, the poor old boy, and me finding him dead on the floor like that. It fair gave me the hab-dabs, I can tell you.'

The door of the Chief Constable's office was open. The bluff, burly, red-faced man sitting behind the solid oak desk looked up, and grimaced a welcome.

'Morning, sir,' Walsh said, drawing up a chair.

'Morning, Sidney,' the C.C. replied, indicating a coffee pot and some cups with a sweep of his hand. 'Help yourself. I gather you've got yourself another case. Professor Higgins, I believe.'

Walsh poured coffee and added milk and sugar. 'That's right. The cleaner found his body in his study. His skull had been fractured by blows to the back of the head. There was no sign of the weapon used. Packstone's people have got all the samples they want, but I don't think we're going to learn anything of great value, unless we're very lucky. The last person to have used the study light switch wore gloves, and went out of the front door. Mrs Higgins made prints over the smudges when she came home. There's no sign of forced entry either, and the cleaner, who's got her own key, found all the other outside doors were locked, as usual. Nothing appears to have been taken, though, that's the strangest thing. What else? Packstone and the doctor reckon Higgins was leaning over his computer when he was struck down, and his assailant was of less than average height – but whether male or female, is anyone's guess.' He paused to sip his coffee.

'I think I might have met this Higgins fellow. Was he a tall, thin man, getting on for sixty or so?' the C.C. asked.

'Yes, that's him. A physicist at Downing College. I had a short chat with his wife yesterday, but she came over queer after a while, so I've left her alone. She'd been out to a party of some sort the night before and didn't get back until the early hours. Not much of a marriage, by all accounts. Higgins appears to have been almost totally absorbed in his work. I learned more from gossiping with the cleaner, separate bedrooms, snappy conversations, arguments, things like that. Higgins regularly took their dog for a walk in the evenings, round the meadows down by the river. Sheeps Green it's called, although I've only ever seen cows on it. You know where I mean? He did so that night, and was seen by several people. They've got just the one son, in business out Royston way. Each of them has got pots of money, apparently. Mrs Higgins thought his only enemies would be professional rivals, so I'll get a list of those from his college.'

'You say he was a Downing man?' the C.C. asked thoughtfully. 'In that case I suppose you'll be talking to that Professor Hughes fellow. He probably knows more of what goes on in the University than anyone else.'

'That's right, I get on well with him. He talks a lot of

sense. You know I'm a bit short of people on the ground, don't you? Particularly with Finch away on that course. I'm having to use young Brenda Phipps as a Number Two, and I've co-opted some of the uniformed men to do some of the running round. I can manage, but don't expect miracles. If the motive turns out to be related to Higgins's work, this might turn out to be an interesting case.'

'Results don't always depend on the amount of man-power you can throw at a problem, Sidney. You'll have to manage with the people you've got, unless you want to call Finch off his course. Now, I'm in London all day tomorrow, so come and see me the day after, and you can tell me then how things are going.'

'How did you get on at Councillor Stevens'?' Brenda asked Constable Myres.

'Not too bad. A real posh place they've got there, you know. They've even got a maid! In this day and age, too. I've never seen one in real life before, they must have pots of money.'

'So! What did they have to say?'

'It was like you said. They did have a big party the night before last, "reception", they called it. Old Stevens is on the board of a charity that was set up way back, helping orphans and neglected children in the Sudan. Pity they can't do more, closer to home. Anyway they give these parties and expect their guests to make a contribution to the charity. Nice if you can afford it.'

'But what did they have to say about Mrs Higgins?' asked Brenda, impatiently.

'I'm going to write my report now, as a matter of fact. Oh well, if you insist. After a lot of humming and ha-ing between old Stevens and his missus, seems they had a lot of people turn up and all three rooms downstairs were pretty well filled up by nine o'clock. Mrs Higgins was early, earlier

24

than usual, they said, but neither of them, or the maid, can remember seeing her after tennish.' Myres added hastily, seeing an angry glint coming into Brenda's eyes, 'But they're not really sure. She could have gone earlier, or been in the loo and gone later.'

'Do your report, and get a copy to the Chief as soon as you can,' Brenda said.

'If Mrs Higgins's got a lover then we've got to know all about him, Brenda,' Walsh said, tapping his teeth with his pipe stem. 'Maybe the old eternal triangle rears its ugly head again. You'd better go yourself to Councillor Stevens' place and find out everyone who attended his party. Then set Myres to seeing them and finding out the exact time she did leave. You'll have to think up some good reason for taking so much interest, or the gossip-mongers will start putting two and two together; next minute it'll be all over town that we think that she did her old man in, so take care what you say. I'll be at Downing College this afternoon seeing our old friend Hughes. It mightn't be a bad thing if you dropped in and had a word with Mrs Higgins on your way out to the Stevens' house. Tell her that tomorrow afternoon would suit us better for a meeting, and we'd like to see the Professor's "Last Will and Testament" when we come. If she hasn't got a copy herself, find out who the solicitor is, and we'll get one from him. Tomorrow morning, at nine, we'll do a brief review of the case, here in my office. Get together all the reports you can, hopefully forensic will have their preliminary findings ready, and chase up our computer friend as well. Maybe we'll be able to see where we want to go next. All right?'

The porter in the college lodge had been forewarned of his coming. Walsh was escorted across a quadrangle and up a

25

short flight of stairs to a varnished mahogany door with a small brass plate on which was engraved, in delicate italics, the name 'Edwin Hughes'.

Hughes was a short tubby man, with a bald head and a relaxed, friendly face. He wore baggy brown corduroy trousers, a checked green shirt, buttoned at the wrists, and a bright red velvet waistcoat with shiny brass buttons. His welcoming smile was genuine, and with obvious pleasure he ushered Walsh into a large room containing a bewildering collection of fine, highly polished mahogany furniture and several high-backed leather armchairs. Oil paintings adorned the walls and the floor was covered with a richly coloured Persian carpet.

'It's a pity the circumstances necessitating your visit are unhappy ones, Inspector, but sit down and have coffee with me.' Hughes's friendly voice was deep and resonant.

'That's very kind of you. I'd like that,' Walsh admitted.

Hughes fetched a tray from a kitchen annexe.

Walsh relaxed into one of the chairs with a sigh of pleasure. 'I suppose you professors make yourselves excessively comfortable so that you can think properly. Mind you, just to enter a college, or a church for that matter, seems to neutralize extraneous thoughts. Handy for concentrating,' he murmured, partly to himself, as he sipped the coffee from a delicately painted porcelain cup.

'That's very true, although by will-power the mind can be freed, whatever the physical surroundings, but I agree, it's certainly easier in comfortable ones. I don't think I'm the type to be a hermit in a cold, draughty cave,' Hughes replied, with another deep chuckle.

He had in his hand a brown file, which he leaned forward to hand to Walsh. 'That's a copy of poor Higgins's personnel record file. I'm not sure that it will be of any great use to you, but you might just as well have it anyway. I'll tell you about him. In his field he was a brilliant man, with an original thinker's mind, not that common among learned intellectuals. Higgins was mainly concerned with tutorial work, though, and at that he was particularly good. You might think that's surprising, since he was, perhaps, excessively single-minded, but he did have the gift of communicating meaning to those familiar with his terminology. He was probably quite content with his life, but I don't think happiness was a word that he would have really understood. Still, there you are, the world would be a strange place if we were all too alike.'

'You mean he was a loner, don't you? Did that make him unpopular?' Walsh asked.

'Not in the sense that he was disliked, rather that he was just not popular. He was never actually rude to anybody, not to my knowledge anyway, but he could be very off-putting. People did tend to try and avoid him, but he was quite unconscious of it all. I am trying to be honest with you. It is a little difficult to talk about a respected colleague of such long standing, but you understand what I am trying to convey, I'm sure.'

'Yes, I do. I've already had an indication of the kind of man he was from his wife.'

Hughes nodded understandingly. 'Yes, that was not a happy relationship either; however, to a certain extent they each drew some benefit from the other. From his point of view she provided stability and regular order in his life, although a good housekeeper would have done that just as well. She, on the other hand, had an introduction into a stratum of society that suited her well, even if she wasn't an intellectual herself. I imagine in the early days of the marriage there must have been some affection; they did have a son, and I've always thought of her as a very pleasant woman, but undoubtedly one starved of affection. I never felt that her involvement in charitable work made up for it. Their son was a disappointment to him certainly, possibly to them both. The boy was sent to boarding school, naturally, so she never really had the chance to unleash her pent-up affections on him. The truth of the matter is, let's be honest, Higgins was the type of man that ought never to have been married. He should have been cloistered from birth, then he could have been devoted to his single-mindedness without hurting anyone else. I've never had the slightest hint that Madge Higgins looked elsewhere for love and affection, but that doesn't mean she didn't.'

Hughes paused to pour himself another cup of coffee, then handed the pot to Walsh.

'Can you suggest any other kind of motive?' Walsh asked. 'Mrs Higgins thought that there were a number of people who envied him his reputation, or might be keen to learn his latest research, whatever that may be. What's your opinion? Is this an area that could arouse enough strength of feeling to cause the death of a man?' Walsh watched with interest the expressions on the shrewd face of the man opposite.

'Now you're putting me on the spot, aren't you? Well, it would depend on how some people saw Higgins's work, relative to their own.' He grinned as he saw the slightest flicker of a smile touch the corners of Walsh's mouth. 'It may surprise you, but Higgins's pet subject was "sound". Sound and its relationship with animal and human behaviour. Warning cries, "feed me" sounds, anything that triggered an inherited, instinctive reaction. He had several papers on that published in technical journals, and was involved in correspondence with many people, world-wide. There have been occasions when he has refuted the opinions of others and been proved to be correct.' Hughes slipped his hand into an inside pocket of his startlingly red waistcoat and brought out a sheaf of papers, which he leaned forward to hand to Walsh. 'There you are, Inspector. A preliminary list of those people that might fall into that category, with the reasons why I have included them.'

Walsh was taken by surprise. 'But you only knew I was

coming this morning,' he almost stuttered. 'You couldn't possibly have known what questions I would ask.'

'On the contrary, I've had since yesterday afternoon, when I first heard of poor Higgins's death. True, I didn't know it was you who would be coming, but I knew someone would, and if they were any good at their job, they would ask me these questions. Why are you so surprised?' Hughes smiled broadly at Walsh's consternation, then set out, quite happily, to add to it. 'Now listen carefully to what I have to say. He was working privately on a little project of his own, to do with his hobby. He was trying to create a combination of those sounds known to penetrate into the subconscious, to calm disturbed human minds, and he was having some success. I know he had an experimental prototype machine built that worked to some degree . . .' Hughes paused again, for dramatic effect. '. . . but I must impress on you that there is an element of security in this project. A government department was extremely interested in his theories in relation to riot control, and, of course, well, there could have been military applications as well. Imagine troops in a bayonet charge suddenly losing their aggressive inclinations. His project was known only to very few people, and it would be better if it remained that way. On that sheet of paper is a telephone number. If you ring that you may learn about the official side of his work. Higgins made use of the services of two laboratory technicians to help with the construction of the prototype. Their names are also on that paper. He analysed the sounds of several pieces of music as well as his bird cries. Amazingly similar, I remember him telling me, the hidden undertones in "Abide with me" and "Go to sleep my baby". In addition to that, he analysed the voices of two hypnotists. Their names are also written down for you. At close range, that prototype gadget could effectively suspend the thought processes of some ninety-eight people out of a hundred. I do think, Inspector, that you should ascertain whether that

29

machine is still in the house of Professor Higgins. If it is not, then I, personally of course, believe you may have found at least one motive for his murder.'

He obviously found the expression on Walsh's face to be amusing, since he gave another of his deep, rumbling chuckles.

4

'So! Someone did the old man in, then. Was there much missing? I hope they didn't take that little woodland picture in the dining-room, that's worth a pretty penny.' The short, rather plump son of Professor Higgins had fair hair, smoothed straight back from his forehead, and creases round his mouth that formed a constant ironic smile.

'It appears that nothing has been taken,' Brenda Phipps replied, glancing again round the room in the house near Royston. Untidy was too mild a word; books, papers, video cassettes, articles of clothing, all lay about in confusion, and there was dust on the baby grand piano that dominated the far end of the long room.

'You mean they bashed him on the head and ran off without pinching anything?' John Higgins said incredulously. 'That's unusual, isn't it? Perhaps they were disturbed by someone. I suppose that's the angle you'll be working on,' he surmised.

Brenda shrugged her shoulders non-committally.

'It sounds more as though one of the downtrodden masses has struck a decisive blow against the rich and privileged; and good luck to him. The universities are a particularly evil bastion of male domination and class establishment, just as the likes of you are.' John Higgins's slim, pallid wife, Vanessa, in her shapeless, long black dress, looked accusingly at Brenda.

'Were you aware of anyone holding a grudge against your father, or any reason why someone might have wanted him dead?' Brenda asked.

John Higgins thought for a moment, then the grin broadened. 'Yes!' he said, his face reddening slightly. 'Me! I'll love the old boy a damned sight more now he's dead than ever I did while he was alive. Won't I, darling? So long as he didn't change his will, that is.'

'I've not the slightest interest in your father's filthy capitalist money, John, as you know well,' Vanessa said off-handedly.

'You didn't say that when we set up all those rallies and that newspaper with it the other year.'

'That was a different matter. We set out to show the working masses the way to freedom. It was ironic that we used the funds of a blatant capitalist.' Her eyes glinted coldly as she fingered the rows of beads hanging round her neck.

'Did you visit your father regularly?' Brenda inquired.

'I'd see him occasionally, when I went to see my mum, about once a month or so. It depends on my business commitments, you see.'

'What line of business are you in?'

John Higgins hesitated and looked thoughtful. 'I do a bit of importing and exporting, mostly in the sports and entertainment fields.'

'Your father helped you get going, did he?'

'Not this time, he didn't. He'd chipped in in the past, but the miserable old sod wouldn't help me on this one, and some of the franchises cost a fair old packet, you know, so did the stock. It was my old mum who coughed up the readies when needed, bless her heart, didn't she, dear?'

'It was your mother's duty to help her son in time of need but a more useless, mindless parasite on society, I have never met. Dreadful,' Vanessa said dismissively.

'Would you mind telling me what you were doing and

where you were the night before last?' Brenda asked, turning a page of her notebook.

'That's easy. We were both at home here, all evening. I don't remember if we had any visitors that night. No, I don't think so. Just a quiet evening on our own, watching telly, reading and playing the old joanna over there. That's all.'

'Sure I got your message, but really, I think you must be joking, Brenda,' said the uniformed sergeant in charge of the lost bicycles warehouse. 'Just look at all this lot.' He waved his arm vaguely towards the assorted mass of machines that nearly filled the room. 'Two sales a year, just to get rid of the darned things. This year's worse than normal. We'll have to start piling them on top of each other, or we won't be able to move in here, and you want to find a particular bike that might or might not have been stolen. What do you look for? Just tell me that,' he demanded.

'Yes, yes, I understand that, Sarge, but the Inspector thinks that the killer of Professor Higgins came and went on a bike, possibly a stolen one. We've got to check.'

'Maybe, but there's little I can do to help. What I've done is to list those bikes reported stolen the day before, that day and the day after, and all the bikes we found abandoned. One or two match up and the owners'll be here to collect any time now. Anyway, I've put them all in that room over there. There's twenty. I don't know what you're going to do with them, but I'd appreciate your not taking too long over it. I need the space.'

Brenda took the list, and spent an hour looking at the bicycles in the room, then pursed her lips, shrugged her shoulders and went off.

'I did a fair bit of rushing about yesterday evening, Brenda,' Walsh said, leaning back in his chair and starting to fill his pipe.

He told her of his conversation with Professor Hughes at Downing College, about Professor Higgins's project.

'You say that this prototype machine is black, and a bit bigger than a old box Brownie camera, Chief?' Brenda asked.

'Yes, that's about right, but we didn't find it in the house. I had a search team go right through the place, but it wasn't there. I saw the cleaning woman again, and she remembers seeing something that fits the description, in Higgins's study, that very morning. So we've got to assume the killer took it, and that possibly he was after the data in the computer. Hughes's list of professional rivals has got to be taken very seriously too.' He took a long puff of his pipe and then put it down on the desk.

'It broadens the whole field, doesn't it, Chief? I mean, as you said, that black box could be very useful, and it has military potential.'

'That's right,' he replied, thinking of some of the scenes of angry violence he'd faced in days gone by, and how a press of a switch on a machine like that might have brought things to a peaceful conclusion. A lot of injuries and mental problems could have been avoided. 'So, we've got to find out all those who knew of its existence, for starters. It's top secret, you appreciate that.'

'Of course,' Brenda acknowledged.

'Good. It means a slight restriction on our freedom of movement. That government department can't rule out the possibility of espionage and will be taking steps of their own, checking on the kind of people they are always keeping an eye on. There's nothing much in all these reports for us to go on yet,' he said, tapping the pile of papers with the back of his hand. 'The patrol cars saw nothing, they never do. Stolen bikes? There's always dozens, every day. Why people can't lock them up properly, I'll never know. No fingerprints, the killer used black cotton gloves. Well, I didn't expect much, so I can't be disappointed, can I? Now

34

you didn't take to the Higgins boy's wife, I gather. Why not?'

'That's right, I didn't. She's a real left-wing bitch. As nasty a piece of work as I've ever met. I've never come nearer to losing my temper. I didn't think much of him either, but how he can put up with her, I don't know. Weird pair, not much to choose between them. He visited his mother only last week, so it's possible he could have known about his father's project.'

'Well, he stays on the suspect list. Now, we've a fair bit to do. You're going to see some of the people on the Stevens' guest list, aren't you? I'd like you to do these two laboratory assistants as well, while I go out to see this female hypnotist that lives out at Sawston. We can meet up at the Higgins place at two thirty, and we'll do Mrs Higgins together. OK?'

'Yes, but there's something I want to do before I go out, though, Chief,' Brenda replied thoughtfully.

'Haven't you gone yet? For Pete's sake, Brenda, what the devil are you reading up on "Prowlers and Peeping Toms" for? We've got a murder case on our hands that needs all our attention,' Walsh said irritably, when he returned to his office half an hour later.

'It's relevant, Chief,' she replied, quite unabashed.

'How come? We've always got prowlers. Each year brings a new batch of randy undergrads. First thing they do is ask the way to Girton College. Harmless enough, most of them. No trouble, as long as they keep their hands to themselves, sort of thing, and I'm not so sure that some of those girls don't get a kick out of being peeped at when they've got nothing on.'

'Maybe so, Chief, but it's Higgins's black box hypnotizer that interests me at the moment. Do you remember the girl with that Hell's Angels group, that ended up in hospital after they chased a prowler? Well, she thought he had a black box, so I'm just looking through the file, and there was a fellow chased out of Homerton College's grounds the other night. He'd got a camera or box-like thing, too.'

Walsh looked thoughtful, and rubbed his chin. Descriptions given of fleeting glimpses at night were bound to contain cliché phrases. 'A camera' was too positive; 'a black box' was sufficiently vague. But Brenda was right, though: coincidences had to be checked, even if it turned out to be just a turn of phrase. 'The average prowler doesn't take a camera with him at night, though. To use it effectively he'd need a flash, and I'm not being funny, but that'd be risky,' he mused aloud.

'He might be a "dirty photo" man, Chief, after something original that he can sell. Alternatively, if it was Higgins's black box, then he might have been planning to use its hypnotic power on some unsuspecting girl. Then who knows what might happen?'

'It's a thought. Now, we sent someone on a pornography familiarization course recently. Sergeant Smith, I think it was. Have a word with him, he should be genned up on the latest prowler psychology.'

'I don't know about the Homerton College set-up, but a video of a Hell's Angels' gang bang would be worth a packet on the porn market, Brenda,' Sergeant Smith said with a smile, handing her back the 'prowler' file.

'I hadn't thought about the camera being a video one,' Brenda admitted.

'Oh yes, that's where the big money is, and the market is international and vast. The dealers all have personal contacts, you see. It's a bit like the drugs racket, no need to advertise. Distribution centre, Amsterdam. It's quality and originality makes the difference between the exceptional

36

and the mundane. I don't mean quality in the technical sense, but quality in the genuineness of the set-up. They can do these things with actors, of course, but the results lack the spice of reality that turns those sort of people on.' Smith lit a cigarette and leaned forward on the desk. 'Now your Hell's Angels' bang, I think that could be a real winner. It's got just about everything, leather gear and studs, powerful motor bikes and callous brutality, to go with the bare flesh and the sex. Mighty risky, but well worth it if you could get it on tape, I should have thought.'

'But those girls are all doing it willingly, aren't they? Wouldn't it be all a bit too easy, and tame?'

'I've never seen one, myself, but knowing some of those guys I wouldn't have thought so. They're not the gentlest of folk at the best of times, and when they're out to demonstrate their virility as well as their toughness, anything could happen. Look at it from the girl's point of view. It don't sound much when you say it quickly, but with those blokes coming at her, one after the other, well, she might well find she'd bitten off more than she could chew. But there'd be no stopping it then, and if she struggled it'd be like stirring up a wasps' nest. I'm only a bloke, so I don't know what it'd be like. The wife of one of the Roman Caesars liked them big, tough and often. Didn't she take on a local whore, to see who could have the most in a day? But what I mean is, it probably takes a bit of practice to get to that stage. No, I'd reckon the girl'd get knocked about a bit – spicy stuff for the perverted mind. But as I say, mighty risky. I'd hate to think what might happen to someone caught spying by those fellows. Likely lose more than just a spot of blood.'

'But you think it would be worth the risk, commercially, if it came off? Despite being shot at night in poor light, presumably using a zoom lens?'

'Be worth a hell of a lot to someone with contacts in the

market, and there's ways of enhancing the picture quality, if you've got the right equipment.'

Brenda stared down at her fingernails. 'Someone must have learned the Hell's Angels' plans, and was prepared to take the risk. Do you think he'd do it again, if he had the opportunity?' she asked.

Smith looked alarmed. 'What are you thinking, Brenda? For Christ's sake don't get involved. Those motor-cycle groups can get real nasty, and they don't like us.'

Brenda looked at him slyly, from under her long eye-lashes. 'You wouldn't let a poor girl tackle this sort of thing on her own, now would you?'

'Come off it, Brenda. Drop it. The Inspector would go barmy if he knew you were trying to set up something like that,' Smith protested.

'He doesn't need to know. Now does he?'

'How do you mean Mrs Higgins didn't seem her normal self? In what way?' Brenda asked the tall, horsey-faced woman with the haughty, supercilious manner.

'Well, she usually got in with a group of her particular friends, and stayed with them all evening, but the other night she was much more animated, moved about from group to group quite quickly. She laughed a lot too, loudly at times, calling attention to herself. Quite unlike her usual behaviour, and she'd got more colour in her face, which made me think she'd started drinking even earlier that evening. I notice things, you see, but I've nothing against her, you understand. I don't particularly like her, mind you. She's got about as much life in her as a wet, boiled rag, and her conversation is just about as interesting. What the Professor ever saw in her, I do not know, such an in-telligent, generous man too. We'll miss him. His death's a terrible tragedy. I can't understand why anyone should want to harm him. Such a loss. He could always be relied on

38

to contribute to any charity, when I asked him. So kind and understanding, too.'

'Did Mrs Higgins have any particular male friends? Her husband never seems to have accompanied her to any of these functions.'

'I doubt it, I've got more sex appeal in my little finger than she's got in the whole of her body, in spite of all her make-up, and wearing flimsy clothes that are much too young for her, just to show off her figure. A real man would get more response from a blow-up doll than from her. Insipid, she is.' Her long nose wrinkled with disdain. 'The Professor must have given up years ago, poor old chap; and she's never responded to any of the girls in the gang, either, not that I'd fancy her even if she had. Still you never know, do you? Quiet waters run deep. Do you think it was her that did it? I mean, you're asking an awful lot of questions about her, so you must think it's likely. I wouldn't have thought she'd got it in her, myself.'

'You didn't happen to see Mrs Higgins leave, the other night, did you? If you did, I'd like to know what the time was,' Brenda inquired, concentrating her gaze on the point of her pencil.

'So you do think that, don't you? Well, well, well, we could have a real scandal in our midst.' She rubbed her hands together in delight.

'Our inquiries are just routine. It's a procedure we have to follow. You shouldn't draw any false conclusions. Did you see her leave?'

'Well, not exactly, but I did see her go out of the drawing-room into the lounge. It would have been about nine, then. She wasn't there when I went in myself, about an hour later. Is that any help?'

'Can you remember the names of some of the people in the lounge when you got there?'

'Some of them. Let me think now.'

5

Marion Dubonnet showed Walsh into her sitting-room. She was a pretty, dark-haired woman, about forty years old, with beautiful, bright blue eyes and a soft, slightly husky voice, sweet and mellow.

'Yes, of course I remember Professor Higgins,' she replied to his question. 'A nice man, although I didn't think so at first, not until I understood what he was really after. He wanted to record my voice during sessions, you see. Well, none of us are particularly keen on that sort of thing, but a friend of mine, who works in the University, checked up on him for me, and it turned out that he was a specialist with animal warning cries. So then I knew what he was up to.'

'How do you mean? What's the connection?' asked Walsh, innocently.

'Warning and feeding cries are instinctive, you see. They're not learned after birth, they form part of the sub-conscious, the built-in brain patterns that are inherited. It's a popular theory that hypnotism creates a direct link with those initial behaviour brain circuits, when the patient's conscious mind is temporarily switched off. It's a nice idea, because it explains so much of what actually happens, but who knows for certain? I can drive a car, but I don't fully understand what's happening under the bonnet. Anyway, that's the theoretical link with animal behaviourism.' She smiled at Walsh. Her eyes were a rich blue, deep and unfathomable. Nice eyes, it was a pleasure to look at them. 'So I did some sessions for him,' she continued, her voice becoming slightly more husky. 'I needed the money, you see. The Professor was a very kind man, particularly when he understood my situation.'

Walsh's eyes asked a silent question.

'Yes.' Her face showed a flicker of despair. 'Mine is the only income we've got now. My husband is upstairs, he's been bed-ridden now for three months. He's dying, there's nothing can be done for him, and he hasn't got long to live. But I won't let him go into hospital. I owe him so much for the years we've been married and I'll stay with him until the end. Then I'll face the world as best I can, without him.' Her eyes became watery, but she blinked back the tears. 'We've no children, unfortunately, they would have been a help at this time. However you're not interested in my problems, are you? We were talking about Professor Higgins, weren't we? He came to three or four sessions with his recording gear, and seemed very satisfied with the results. He paid me a hundred and fifty pounds for that. A lot more than it was worth, but I didn't protest. Perhaps I should have done, but he would probably have insisted anyway. He mentioned that he needed to record a male voice as well, to confirm the frequency change patterns, so I assumed from that, that the pitch of the sounds was not of such a great importance as the sequence of the changes themselves,' she said thoughtfully.

'So as far as you are aware then, Professor Higgins merely wanted these recordings as part of his general researches? Did he mention anything more specific?'

'No, I don't think so. What sort of thing did you mean?' Her expressive eyes darkened with curiosity.

'Nothing in particular. So what does your hypnotism work generally entail?'

'I work mostly in the evenings. My clients are usually

41

people trying to give up smoking or wanting to lose weight. The rest come under the heading of phobias, worry or lack of confidence. Sessions can last for an hour and a half, two hours, something like that. Quite often I do the smokers in groups of four or five. They seem to feel happier if others are suffering as well as themselves,' she replied, with half a grin. 'I suppose I must be on your suspect list for you to be asking me all these questions. Why, I can't imagine. Still that doesn't matter, let me see if I have an alibi.' She rose from the floral-patterned armchair and walked over to a small reproduction oak bureau, a lithe figure in tight, well-washed blue jeans and a fluffy, many-coloured woollen sweater. She opened a drawer and brought out a thick diary. 'Which day are you interested in?' she asked.

'The day before yesterday, in the evening.'

'Well, that's all right then. I had three consecutive sessions that evening, from five o'clock until eight.'

'So your last client left about half-past nine,' he suggested.

'Perhaps a little later than that. The last session consisted of three reluctant smokers. I don't suppose I got rid of them much before ten.'

'May I look at your diary, please?' Walsh requested, holding out his hand for the book.

She handed it to him without a word, but frowned, nevertheless.

'This is a murder inquiry, everything must be checked, until the matter is resolved,' he explained as he turned the pages.

It was a normal appointment diary. Walsh wrote down the names and addresses of her clients for that evening in his notebook, then closed it, and handed the diary back.

'Thank you for seeing me this morning, Mrs Dubonnet. I appreciate your help, and I'm sorry to have had to bother you,' he told her, holding out his hand.

The blue eyes that watched his face flashed momentarily as her warm hand touched his.

'I know something of how his wife must be feeling, losing her husband so suddenly, without warning. She must be quite devastated, poor woman,' she said sincerely.

Walsh walked thoughtfully back to his car. He felt slightly light-headed for some reason, as though he'd had just one glass too many, but his mind was already pondering the contrasts between this woman and the one he was now to go and see.

There were similarities in height and build, but they were a world apart in personality and attitude to life. The one he was just leaving – a little reluctantly, he would have liked to have stayed longer – was active and loving, bravely facing up to reality, in spite of the prospect of a bleak, lonely future. The other, bored by her comfort and wealth, in comparison appeared to lack any real enthusiasm for life.

'All right?' Walsh asked Brenda, as they walked together over the gravel drive, to the front door of the Higgins' house.

'Yes, but I only saw one of Higgins's lab assistants, I'm afraid, the other hadn't turned up for work. I'll have to go round and see if I can find him at home later,' she replied.

Mrs Higgins looked tired and nervous, but Walsh could find no sympathy for this woman, not with Marion Dubonnet still in his mind. He tried to be impartial, but his opening words came out a little more stiffly than he had intended. 'I hope you're feeling better today, Mrs Higgins.'

'Yes I am, thank you, Inspector. I feel much better today,' she replied coolly.

'We're still looking for a satisfactory motive for your husband's murder. Do you have a copy of his will?' Walsh asked.

Mrs Higgins walked over to the fireplace, took a long

43

brown envelope from the mantelpiece and gave it to him. 'It also contains a preliminary schedule of my husband's assets, but there are pension fund benefits and insurance policies to be added yet,' she said tonelessly.

Walsh removed the contents from the envelope, and spread them out on his lap.

The will was relatively short, containing perhaps a dozen or so bequests. The first was one of a hundred and fifty thousand pounds to Downing College. Then came a list of individual names, with bequests of various sums ranging from five to fifty thousand. Walsh's eyes blinked with surprise at the name next to the highest figure: Marion Dubonnet. He tried not to show his surprise. The house with its contents, and one hundred and fifty thousand pounds, were left to Higgins's wife, and all the residue to his son.

The last sheet, typed out on the solicitor's letter-heading, contained a note stating that the valuations of Professor Higgins's assets were provisional estimates for probate purposes only. There followed a list of share holdings, bank and building society accounts. The total, including a valuation of the house and contents at five hundred thousand pounds, came to over one million, four hundred and fifty thousand pounds. And that, thought Walsh, excludes insurance policies. A tidy sum, and a tidy number of motives as well.

'My husband's grandfather was a very wealthy man, and Robert was his sole heir,' Mrs Higgins explained.

'Was he, indeed? Your son John inherits the bulk of your husband's estate. He's in business himself, I understand. To what extent was he financed by yourself or your husband?' he asked.

'My son made several unsuccessful attempts to start a business. For the first few, my husband provided the capital, but then he became convinced that the boy was being indolent and careless, and, unfortunately, he also found out that some of his money had financed the left-wing activities of John's wife. After that, he refused to help any more. There were no unpleasant scenes, my husband was not like that. He just became cold towards John, ruthlessly cold. They spoke when they met, but otherwise my son's existence was ignored. My husband would not make allowances, he was heartless, and very cruel,' she said bitterly.

'But I understand he was quite a generous man,' Walsh interrupted softly.

Mrs Higgins's eyes flashed coldly at him. 'He was weak with some people that he mistakenly thought of as "valiant fighters against adversity"; for an intelligent man he was particularly susceptible to a soft touch. It's a pity he didn't have the same sort of understanding for his own flesh and blood.'

'But here', Walsh tapped the copy of the will with the back of his hand, 'he is, leaving John several hundred thousand pounds. Surely that must show he had some affection for him?'

'I don't think so. That was his duty. He was always a stickler for his stupid honour and his duty. He should have supported his son better. The boy was only trying to make his mark in the world, in the only way he knew. John was doing his best. I'm sure he was.'

'So you had to support him instead, from your own resources. Did you have to sell some of your securities to do that, or could you manage that out of liquid funds? How much have you invested in his business?' Walsh asked, in a flat dispassionate voice.

'Why all these questions about my son? Surely you can't suspect him? That's ridiculous,' she replied with indignation.

'I'm sorry, Mrs Higgins, but your husband was murdered. We have to pursue every possibility, so I'm afraid we must discuss your son.'

This mollified Mrs Higgins somewhat. 'Well, yes, I suppose you must, but it seems such a waste of time. Yes, I did have to sell some of my shares. I haven't been so lucky with my investments as Robert was. He used to look after them for me, but ever since he refused to help John, I haven't let him touch anything that was mine. I've done it all myself, but as I've said, I wasn't as lucky as he was. I suppose I've given my son between twenty or thirty thousand pounds over the past two years, something like that. It's not important, I'm still a wealthy woman, you know.'

'But not as wealthy as you used to be, obviously. However, while we're on the subject, what were your son's feelings towards his father, after all this?' Walsh asked.

'He was hurt by it, of course he was. You see, my son was never an academic like his father. He rather took after me, more artistic. He never managed to get into college. For some people, finding their proper role in society is not straightforward, nor is it easy. They need to try a variety of things before they become settled. Robert couldn't understand this. He convinced himself that John was good for nothing, he called him a layabout, but it isn't true. He's a good boy. I know he is,' she added with something like a sob.

'How often did he visit you here and how often did you visit him and his wife in Royston? It's not far away.'

'Now you really are getting nasty, Inspector. I know you say you are only doing your job, so I'll try not to take offence, but you really are making it difficult for me to be polite. My son's wife, unfortunately, considered that I was a member of the capitalist establishment, and as a result was unable to allow my visits to pass without becoming uncivil. I can understand her deep devotion to a cause and so I was never rude in return, but I obviously wasn't welcome there. So it's several years since I visited them, but he does come and see me regularly.'

'How often?' insisted Walsh.

'Every month or so. He's very busy, you understand, Inspector,' she answered lamely.

'You told us, the other day, that on the night your husband was killed, you went off to a party, or a reception I think you called it, at the home of Councillor Stevens, and you arrived back home in the early hours. Mrs Higgins, we know you arrived at the Stevens' house shortly after eight o'clock that evening, but we have also learned that you had definitely left before ten. If you didn't arrive home until gone three in the morning, where did you go between those times?'

'My God, you've been checking up on me, asking my friends questions about me. My God, what will they think? Inspector, this is intolerable.' She rose to her feet, her face reddened with rage and anger, both hands clenched tightly into fists.

'I'm sorry you think that, Mrs Higgins,' Walsh said calmly, 'but you misled us by what you said the other day. Now, I'm afraid I must ask you again. Where were you during that time? We must know. You do realize that, don't you?'

Mrs Higgins glared back at Walsh, her eyes wide and slightly wild, but he held her gaze resolutely and impassively.

After a few moments she regained control over her anger and sat down on the settee again, putting her face into her hands.

'Where were you, Mrs Higgins?' Walsh's voice was now hard and insistent.

'I didn't feel very well at the party,' she replied, quietly. 'I couldn't face going home, so I ... I drove out into the countryside.' She took her hands from her face and stared at Walsh defiantly. 'I'd had too much to drink, so I parked somewhere and slept it off. When I woke up, I drove home. It's as simple as that. Now you're going to ask me where it was I parked. It was out towards Royston, but don't ask me where. I don't remember. Now, I've tried to be reasonable and helpful, but I feel I just can't answer any further

47

questions now. I'm tired, these past few days have been horrible for me. Please leave me alone now.'

Walsh expressed his sorrow at having caused her so much inconvenience and thanked her for her assistance, then he and Brenda left: he to drive slowly and thoughtfully back to his office, while Brenda set off to call on the laboratory assistant who had failed to turn up for work that day.

Walsh had just settled down in his office to write some notes on the day's events, when a telephone call from Brenda was put through.

'I can't get a reply,' she told him, 'but the milk's still outside the door, and the television is on, I can hear it through the letter box. No one has seen him today, Chief. I'm worried. I think something's wrong. I want to get in, but I can't find anyone with a key.'

Walsh's heart beat a little faster.

'Hold your horses, Brenda. Wait for me. What's the address? Right, I'll be with you in just a few minutes.'

6

The bed that morning was warm and comfortable. George Varney stretched himself between the soft cotton sheets. Except for a slight headache he was relaxed and at ease. Today was his day off; there was no need to bustle about and get ready for work.

He turned over and snuggled down again, his mind starting to drift back into that pleasant state of limbo, not really awake or asleep.

Then memories of last night returned. His visitor had brought the black box in a carrier bag. That had been exciting; but there had been bitter disappointment later on. In spite of his pleadings and cajolement, his visitor had refused to get into his bed, and had insisted on sleeping alone, on the couch in the living-room. That had been very unfair, since he'd worked himelf up to such a state of anticipation that his resultant frustration had brought him to tears of desperation, literally. His pathetic exposure of himself while he had pleaded had brought a look of humiliating contempt on the other's face. It had taken several whiskies before sleep eventually came to him in his lonely bed.

He was wide awake now: rising anger had swept away his relaxed contentment. He swung himself off the low divan and pulled the living-room door open.

His visitor had gone, leaving no visible traces.

He hurried to the front window and looked out. As usual the street was full of vehicles, and today being dustman day, it was also lined with untidy piles of blue plastic rubbish bags.

He found his slippers, pulled on a faded green dressing-gown, and took his own plastic bag out of the flip-top rubbish bin, pulling the top into two big ears and tying them together. Then he took the bag downstairs. Outside were two more, from the other flats into which the house was divided.

He searched in the cupboard under the sink for a new liner. The dustmen always left one when they collected the full bags but quite often by the time he got back from work they had all been pinched, or were blowing about in the street. He rummaged around until he found one, and that was how he found the black box, lying behind the Vim, the Ariel and the empty margarine tubs.

He picked it up carefully and laid it on the table. His lips twisted into a wry grin.

So! His visitor hadn't wanted the risk of keeping the box, in case anything went wrong, but obviously there wasn't the slightest concern about him. His teeth gritted in anger at the unfairness of it all. He had been so open, honest and helpful, all he had wanted in exchange was a little love and understanding. Well, at least it did mean that his visitor would be back. Something ought to be done to make his visitor admire him and thus desire to reward him by submitting willingly to his caresses.

He made himself a cup of coffee, and sat down to think. He knew what the box could do. Professor Higgins had tried it out on him. Not that he remembered much of the effects really, he'd felt nothing at all. He had come to his senses slowly, like waking from a deep sleep, and wouldn't actually have known that anything had happened to him had not Higgins been sitting there, opposite him, with his watch in his hand. Ten minutes he'd been under the influence, and Higgins had only given him a burst of short duration.

The time control was the bottom dial on the right-hand side.

He knew Higgins was afraid to use too much volume because it was dangerous, but at ten feet they had shown it to be safe. That box had the power to control people, and in the right place, at the right time, it could be used very profitably; it just needed a bit of thinking about. Then his visitor would appreciate his ingenuity, and his humiliation could be forgotten.

It should be used somewhere where there were not too many people, somewhere quiet but accessible. Out in one of the villages perhaps. That would make sense.

He felt his body stir with excitement. Not only would it impress his visitor, it would also be very, very useful; he was always short of money.

When?

Shops were usually quietest just after lunch, weren't they?

Well, there was no need to hurry. He'd do a bit of shopping first, and get some wine, that would be nice for a celebration tonight.

He took off his large-lensed, gold-framed spectacles and polished them nervously, wishing that he hadn't given up smoking. He could do with a cigarette right now, but he restrained the urge. It had taken a lot of self-control to get this far and he didn't want to go through all that again.

Nothing could go wrong with his plan, surely. He needed to wear gloves, obviously, so that he would leave no fingerprints. He'd better get himelf a pair when he was out.

He finished his coffee and methodically carried out the tasks he had set himself, even changing the sheets and pillow cases on the divan in the bedroom, in happy anticipation. His thoughts travelled more than once to the

51

laboratory where he worked. Electronics was his speciality and he was good at it. That was why he had been recommended to Higgins, for the making up of the miniature computer circuits for the black box. He hadn't known what it was all about then. That wasn't surprising: the boffins rarely took a common lab tech into their confidence. It wasn't until the box was finished that the problem of testing it had suddenly dawned upon Higgins. There could be no secrecy if he had to use a dozen or so human guinea pigs. In his exasperation, Higgins had actually blurted out the problem while Varney was in the room.

'Why don't you try it out on me?' he had offered, thinking that there might be some rewards later on. Higgins had agreed, and carried out the experiment. It was shortly after this that his visitor of last night had started to show some interest in him. His visitor was so graceful and desirable, in spite of the bitterness; it made for a particular fascination. He'd tried to maintain the secrecy that he had sworn to Higgins, but it wasn't long before his acquaintance knew as much about the black box as he did himself, including that little item about the Professor having lost his keys so often that now he always left the front door lock catch up when he took his dog for a walk. He'd learned that when he'd gone to the Professor's house to query an item on the drawings.

He was well aware that his visitor only spoke to him when there was no one else about – that was why he had suggested a visit to his flat. Nevertheless, he had been surprised when the offer had finally been accepted. Now he knew why.

Just before half-past one, dressed in dark clothes and wearing a crash helmet with a front visor, he went out of the back door and wheeled his moped down the side passage to the street.

It was only a few miles out of town to the first village. On

52

the left-hand side of the road was a row of small shops. The middle one was a sub-post office and general store.

His timing was perfect. A rather stout woman had just unbolted the front door and was turning a little sign saying 'Open' to face the outside. By the time Varney had leaned his moped safely against the post-box, she was making her way round to the back of the counter. She turned her head as she heard the door open behind her and a half-smile came on her face, just as he pressed down the button on the black box. Her smile remained fixed, a glazed look appeared in her eyes and she stayed quite still. Varney had to push her aside as he hurried round behind the counter.

His black-gloved finger pressed the key of the shop till, and the drawer swung open. He grabbed all the notes and stuffed them into the front of his windcheater, then turned his attention to the post office corner, behind the metal grilles. The door of a small wall safe hung open. Two steel shelves held postal orders and stamps: he took them. There was a small drawer at the bottom containing bags of coins, which he tossed contemptuously to the floor, but underneath lay several wads of notes. He smiled as he stuffed those in his pockets and hurriedly left the shop, feeling very pleased with himself. He flicked the sign saying 'Closed' round as he shut the door.

It had been so easy; it hadn't taken more than a minute or two from start to finish.

A feeling of recklessness came over him as he rode off, and he threw caution to the wind. During the course of his journey he stopped at three more shops. So bold had he become that he tackled one that actually had a customer in it, as well as the shopkeeper. It all proved dead easy.

Back in his flat his elation almost became hysterical. He pranced about the room giggling to himself in delight. The money fell out all over the floor when he undid his jacket. That provided another excuse for laughter.

He collected it together when he'd calmed down, and

methodically counted it. Not just once, but several times, fingering the notes with as much glee as an actor playing Scrooge with his piles of gold coins.

The notes totalled nearly two and a half thousand pounds, but there were also the postal orders and some cheques he'd taken from the tills. He looked at them dubiously, wishing he'd not taken them. Money couldn't be traced, but these could. So he put them all in a plastic bag and put them in the cupboard under the sink. He was too wound up to go out again today. They could be taken somewhere tomorrow, in some woods perhaps, and burned.

In the mean time he would have a well-deserved cup of coffee and something to eat, after which he would take a bath and relax, watching the television, while waiting for his visitor to return.

So it was, then, that in the early evening Varney lounged on the small settee in his living-room, attired only in his drab green dressing-gown. On the table nearby stood an opened bottle of wine, two glasses, the pile of money and the black box. The other bottle of wine he had put unopened on the dressing-table in the bedroom, for use later on.

But it was not until it had grown quite dark outside, and long after he had had to get up and draw the curtains, both in the living-room and in the bedroom, that a light tap came on the door.

'It's open,' he cried out happily, as he rose to welcome his guest.

The door opened, and the dark-clad figure of his expected visitor stepped inside, pushing the door closed with a click, and then stood still, staring with astonishment at the items on the table.

'I thought you'd be surprised,' he said proudly. 'I've been out using this.' His hand rested on the black box. 'I did a post office and three other shops this afternoon, and I've got nearly two and a half thousand quid. What do you think of that? It was dead easy. Would you care for a glass of wine?'

The other's jaw jutted forward and the eyes became tiny gimlets of outraged fury. 'You stupid, stupid bastard, you might have ruined everything.'

Varney started back with astonishment as the figure moved angrily towards him, hands outstretched, fingers curled like talons.

'I thought you'd be pleased,' he stuttered helplessly. Suddenly he found that he was afraid and both hands came up protectively, his right one still holding the black box. He stared at it, uncomprehendingly, for a moment, then inspiration came to him.

He aimed it and pressed the switch.

The other person stopped coming forward and the facial features relaxed. Varney put the box down on the table. He found he was trembling with emotion. After last night's humiliation, now this as well. He felt anger and hatred, where before there had been devotion.

His visitor stood still and helpless. Now he wasn't afraid. Now there was the temptation to avenge the humiliations of the previous night. His hand reached out to touch the face.

There was no response.

He took an arm and pulled his visitor into the bedroom. For a while he could do whatever he wanted with this person. Anything he liked.

The blood rushed to his face, and his breathing quickened. His hands reached out and fumbled frantically with the buttons and clips, unzipping garments until, at last, the figure could be laid, naked and helpless, on the divan. His hands stroked and caressed the warm, smooth flesh of a softly rounded stomach and firm white thighs. His eyes dwelled wantonly as fingers explored secret places, until he could control his passion no longer. With a lustful, strangled cry, he tore off his own dressing-gown and cast himself down on to the naked body.

Gradually the senses of the visitor returned. Slowly there came a bewildered realization. Incredulity at the lack of clothes, irritation at the hand still lying on the stomach, then outrage at the nakedness of the man lying exhausted on his back alongside, a smug, contented look on his perspiring face. Then blind fury, as the extent of the personal violation that had obviously taken place became clear.

The visitor stood up, trembling, all the hatred for dictatorial authority which exploited the weak and helpless making the eyes redden with madness. The bottle of wine from the dressing-table was seized by the neck, and in one continuous over-arm movement came smashing down on the head of the drowsy man on the divan.

The anger cooled quickly and the figure slowly gathered the crumpled clothes from the floor and dressed. By the time that was accomplished, sanity had completely returned and the figure calmly set about removing all traces of the visit. Gloved hands wiped all the surfaces that might have been touched with a damp cloth and Vim. As a final touch, Varney's wrist-watch was wound on two hours, trodden on, then pushed under the bed.

Varney lay still, naked and motionless, his right temple crushed inwards and his eyes staring sightlessly up at the ceiling.

The visitor made one last check of all the rooms, switched on the television, then quietly slipped out of the door and into the darkness of the night.

7

The squad car sped through the busy streets, its blue light flashing.

'What gives, Inspector?' the plump, uniformed sergeant, now nearing retirement age, asked of his companion in the back seat.

'One of the people we want to talk to on this Higgins case is not answering his door bell. I want you to let us in,' Walsh replied.

'Oh, ah, no problem,' the sergeant said confidently, fingering his little box of locksmith's tools, glad to have escaped for a while from behind his desk and the green computer screen that he spent most of his time watching these days.

There was no room to park. The narrow street was already lined with cars, but that was the driver's problem.

Brenda led the way up the stairs to the narrow landing. 'This is the one, Chief,' she said, standing outside a white, panelled door with a Yale lock.

'Go to it, Sergeant,' Walsh instructed, easing Brenda to one side.

'Piece of cake, sir,' the sergeant replied, selecting a particular tool. He worked it between the door edge and the door jamb, and slid it down to the lock at an angle then, turning the lower door knob, pushed the door open and stood back out of the way.

Walsh stepped inside the living-room, his eyes scanning about intently, but there was no one there. The television was sending out one of its daily round of panel games, the bored presenter with the eternal smile desperately trying to inject some drama into his routine chatter.

But there was plenty of real drama in the small bedroom. Walsh and Brenda looked down at the body of George Varney, lying sprawled and naked on the divan, the eyes staring sightlessly out of the dead white face.

'Ring in, Brenda. Get Packstone's team here,' Walsh muttered hoarsely.

He waited in the living-room, prowling up and down. His confused mind tried to slot this new event into the facts of the case that he already knew, tried to find a pattern, but without success.

Within half an hour the full team had arrived, and after a brief explanation they got to work.

The small rooms were overcrowded. Walsh decided to get out of the way and leave them to it. 'We'll be back in an hour or so,' he said, interrupting Packstone, who was giving instructions to one of his team. 'We're going out to get something to eat. May I use your car, please?'

Packstone dug into his pocket and handed his keys to Walsh. His initial flicker of annoyance at being interrupted was quickly forgotten as he set about his tasks with a methodical enthusiasm.

'Come on, Brenda. We'll go to my place. Gwen'll soon knock us up something. It looks as though we'll be working late again tonight.'

It wasn't a long drive to Walsh's house. His long-suffering wife, Gwen, received the request for a quick meal with a relaxed smile, and the remark that she was getting to be an expert with the microwave anyway.

'At least we can be reasonably sure where the killer got his information about Higgins, now,' Brenda ventured, crushing baked beans on to the back of her fork.

'Very likely,' he agreed.

Gwen brought cups of coffee and sat down at the table to sip at one herself.

'So! You think you'll be working late again, do you?' she asked.

'Looks like it, love. This Higgins case has taken a nasty new twist. I'm afraid that all the stops are going to have to come out now.'

Brenda dropped Walsh off at Headquarters then drove Packstone's car back to the scene of Varney's murder.

Walsh contacted the Chief Constable on the radio phone.

'We've got another body in the Higgins case, one of the lab assistants, I'm afraid. I need a lot of people now,' he said.

'So you want to co-opt other people's teams, do you? How long do you reckon you'll need them?' asked the C.C. gruffly.

'Only for a few days, probably.'

'Right, Sidney, you go ahead. Are you ready for a large-scale briefing?'

'I will be in the morning.'

He called the duty sergeant up to his office.

'I want you to ring the people on this list. They're to drop whatever they're doing and be here with their teams for briefing at six o'clock tomorrow morning, without fail. Got that?'

The sergeant would have a fair bit of work to do to achieve that, but Walsh had little time for sympathy, even if he had thought the occasion warranted any. He rang the training conference centre where Detective Sergeant Finch was on his course, and spoke to the Training Director.

'Sorry, but I need him for at least three or four days. Tell him to get here as soon as he can.' Finch was the best

59

person he knew at routine report reading, and he needed his best team round him now.

He drove his own car back to the street of Victorian houses where Varney had his flat.

Packstone and the team were still busy.

'We'll be a while yet still, Sidney, but I've had them do the living-room first. You can forage around in here to your heart's content. There's only the secret searching to do. We're not getting any prints though. Someone's gone round and made a thorough job of wiping the surfaces clean. Still, you never know what'll turn up.'

'All right, Richard. Brenda and me, we'll just potter around in here, but put a special priority on the processing of this lot, will you? It's a "drop everything else" situation now, and you might well have the vital clue,' Walsh replied quietly.

'It's like that then, is it? I'll have my chaps work through the night, anyway. I'll see you later.' Packstone turned away.

'You look through those kitchen units, Brenda. I'll do this cupboard under the television,' Walsh instructed.

Brenda was the first to make a find of interest.

'Hey, Chief, take a look at this lot,' she cried out excitedly. She turned towards Walsh with a handful of postal orders and a plastic bag, which she tipped out on to the table.

Walsh picked up a couple of cheques. 'This is made out to Hay's Butchers, both of them are. What the hell's this got to do with it all?' he asked loudly.

'Did you say Hay's Butchers, sir?' one of the photographers in the room inquired.

Walsh looked up.

'Yes I did. Why?'

'Well, they got done over yesterday, sir. Funny thing that. No one saw anything.'

'I've not had time to read the log-books today. There was

a robbery at Hay's Butchers yesterday, was there? What about the general store at Coton?'

'Yes, sir, them too. I think you'll find Sergeant Witherspoon went out on them.'

'You said it was a funny thing, what do you mean?'

'Only that nobody remembers seeing anything suspicious, even though the places hadn't been left unattended or so they said. Sergeant Witherspoon told me about it in the canteen before he went off duty. Three or four shops all with the same story. Weird, he reckoned.'

'Right, thank you,' Walsh said, gazing blindly for a moment at nothing in particular. He raised his eyes slowly and looked at Brenda's face.

'Are you thinking what I'm thinking, Chief?' she asked.

'Higgins's hypnotizer, you mean? It could be. If that's the case, it might be here somewhere, although because of what's happened,' he nodded towards the bedroom, 'I very much doubt it. Maybe that's what the killer was after, though.'

'There's no sign of a fight, Chief. Besides, it looked as if there were two head impressions on the pillows in there. Lover maybe, certainly someone intimate. Killer and thief as well, do you think?' Brenda remarked.

'You noticed the pillows then, good. Plenty of time for mental projections later, Brenda. Let's get this place done over. Get Packstone out of the bedroom, see if he has checked these for prints.'

Walsh carried on looking through the papers in the drawers: just bills and statements. Mostly they contained records and tapes, sheet guitar music, journals, pamphlets concerned with electronics, odds and ends; and a half-full packet of cigarettes. Walsh picked the packet up thoughtfully and looked round the room. There were several ashtrays, but each was clean.

Packstone came back into the room. 'We're just finishing up the micro surface samples in the bedroom, then the

61

special search team can do the wardrobe and cupboards again. You've found something interesting, have you? We'll take them back to the lab. We've got the bed cover and pillows as well, we ought to get some skin flakes from them. We've found a small button under the dressing-table. It's too small to be from a man's garment, so there's probably a woman involved, somewhere. Certainly the bed's been romped on. Two glasses set out and a bottle of wine opened, but no meal prepared. Celebration, do you think?' he asked, wiping the lenses of his spectacles.

'Could be,' Walsh replied. 'When you have another look at him, can you see if you can find out if he was, or had been, a smoker? There's this packet of cigarettes, plenty of ashtrays, but no dog ends. I'm intrigued. Brenda, if you've finished, would you go and see the people in the other two flats, and organize someone to start doing calls down the street? They can list all the cars out there first, and check them off as they go round the houses. Find out who owns which. Possibly the killer had a car, if so, it must have been parked somewhere, and someone may have seen it. Ask about bikes as well, then you'd better come back to HQ, I'll need you to help me prepare for the briefing tomorrow. Richard, would you have those cheques and postal orders cleared quickly and sent up to my office? I'll need them as well.' He stood back out of the way, as George Varney's mortal remains were carried out of the bedroom.

Two more figures appeared on the landing and came into the living-room.

'Evening, sir,' said Detective Sergeant Martin Thomas. He, and the constable with him, were the Constabulary's acknowledged search specialists.

Walsh briefed him with the details of this murder. 'I'll leave you to finish up here. Do a good job. If you come across a black box, about a seven-inch cube, with knobs on one side, don't fiddle with it, for Pete's sake. Let me know immediately. In any case, come and see me when you've finished.'

Thomas would miss nothing, under floor-boards, up chimneys. If something had been hidden, it would be winkled out and found.

Walsh walked round each of the rooms in the flat again – he wanted to preserve an accurate mental picture – then left to drive back to his office.

It was a little after eleven o'clock in the evening.

He worked alone at his desk for an hour or so, on the Higgins and the new Varney files, scheduling the action he wanted taken.

Brenda came in at about twelve thirty.

'Varney was a real loner. Very shy, according to the people in the other flats. He didn't seem to have any particular friends, and rarely had any visitors. Frankly, I've learned nothing that might be a lead,' she said ruefully.

'Everything's of some value, even if it's negative. Did his neighbours not see anyone, or hear anything, yesterday evening, then?' Walsh asked.

'Not a thing. They know next to nothing about him, except that he was a good neighbour to have in the middle flat, being quiet and unobtrusive. He dressed a bit scruffy, but kept himself reasonably clean. He kept a moped in a shed in the back garden.'

'Well, I'm taking a break for a few minutes,' he said, getting up and stretching his arms. 'Come and have coffee in the canteen. We can talk some more. I'm sketching out what I want done in general terms. You can backstop me. You'll see the notes I've made. Check me, I don't want to miss anything. You can see if what I want is what you think should be done. When we've done that, we'll do each file in detail, together. OK?'

At about two o'clock, Martin Thomas came in.

'Not a lot to tell you, sir, I'm afraid. The fellow seems to have been just a normal sort of single bloke. Nothing suspicious. No clever hiding places. Just a couple of glossy nude books behind one of the drawers in the bedside cabinet. Nothing weird about them either. I'd say he was one of those lonely guys who wants company but doesn't know how to get it. The kind you see in a pub, drinking on their own but watching everyone that comes in, hoping it might be someone they know. His clothes are reasonably clean without being spotless, same for the pots and pans and things. The only thing that might possibly be of interest is this photograph.' He reached forward over the desk to hand it to Walsh.

It was of a slim person on a blue moped. No features could be seen, since the figure wore a helmet and visor. At the angle the photo was taken the number plates could not be seen.

'For what it's worth I would say that was taken on the old Roman road, up behind the golf course. I found it in the bottom of the wardrobe. It must have been tucked into a clip on the door mirror, you can see a mark on the bottom, so it might be of someone important to him. It looks fairly new, too. I'll get the photo boys to blow it up for you if you like, they're still working,' Thomas offered.

'It could be a lead, and we can't have too many, not at this stage. Do that for me, please. Now I'd appreciate your written report, pronto,' Walsh replied with a slight smile.

Thomas looked at Walsh's face. It was pale and there were signs of strain in the lines round the eyes.

'No problem,' he replied cheerfully. 'No one else is going to get any sleep tonight, so I might just as well stick around and bring myself up to date. You've got me booked for six o'clock, anyway,' he added.

The next visitor knocked tentatively on the door. At Walsh's second shout to come in, one of the junior forensic team opened the door.

'Mr Packstone asked me to bring all these papers up to you, sir,' he said nervously.

'Right, thanks. Leave them there on the desk, please,' Walsh told him.

The young man glanced curiously about the room and at the two serious-looking occupants, but his presence was ignored and, as there seemed to be nothing else required of him, he left, reluctantly. Two murders, and he had only been there three weeks.

About four o'clock the duty sergeant came in.

'Everything's set up as you wanted, sir. The team leaders'll be here at six. I've allowed an hour and a half for your briefing, so the rest of their teams will be ready at seven thirty. I got through to Witherspoon eventually, he'll be here in an hour or so,' he said, thinking that Walsh looked a bit haggard and the woman detective constable certainly wasn't her usual perky self. 'I'll get some coffee and sandwiches sent up, if you like,' he offered.

'You're a grand chap, Sergeant. Make that a couple of fried egg sandwiches, with tomato sauce.'

'I think I can manage that. Any preferences, Brenda?'

'Same for me, please,' she replied, without raising her eyes from the document she was reading.

Packstone came in a little later, while the pair were eating. 'I see. Some of us are working while others are having a picnic. Can anyone join in?' he said humorously as he pulled up a chair and sat down. 'Disappointing news, I'm afraid. There are no prints other than Varney's about the place, but as I told you earlier, someone had gone over all the likely areas with a cloth, with Vim on it. Whoever did that wore black cotton gloves, the kind a woman might wear. We're checking to see if the fibres are the same as those we found in the Higgins' place. There are skin flakes on the bed cover, as you'd expect, but we're still analysing them. That'll take a while, but we might have some identifying agents there, if you can come up with a suspect.

65

Talking about sex, there had been a romp on the bed. It looks as though Varney was killed immediately afterwards – perhaps you're after a female spider who wasn't hungry. What else have I got? Ah yes, the button we found under the dressing-table. Too small to have come from any of Varney's clothes, more like a woman's blouse button, smudged prints on it. Varney's broken watch was found under the bed, hands showed just after midnight, same smudged prints. I don't think you should rely on that time, frankly. I think it's a crude attempt to plant a false lead. I really can't see someone as meticulous as this accidentally treading on it and leaving it there. The pathologist will be putting an approximate time of death at an hour or two before then. Death was caused by a single, very hefty blow, which crushed in the skull, high up on the right temple. The weapon was that bottle of wine. Lastly, Varney's prints are on some of those cheques and postal orders. There are some others too, but they're probably the shopkeeper's and whoever wrote them out, so we'll need to get comparative prints, to be sure. I had a print check done on his moped too. His were the only ones.'

'Ah, good. I'm glad you did that, Richard. What colour was his moped?' Walsh asked.

'Red, why?'

'Thomas found a photo of someone on a blue moped. It was in the bottom of his wardrobe,' Walsh replied, rubbing his hand over his now dark and bristly chin.

'Varney seems to have had remarkably few friends, from the sound of it. Do you want me at your briefing, Sidney? Not much point in me going to bed now,' Packstone offered.

'That's very good of you. Yes, I'd appreciate that.'

Walsh watched the door close as he went out. He'd known Packstone for many years now. He was a brilliant scientist, capable of a more important appointment than the one he held, but as far as Richard Packstone was concerned, ambition was subordinated to life-style. He liked his work, and the stimulating intellectual company of his many friends. Even so, Walsh suspected, being confined to the laboratory was irksome, when a major investigation was in progress.

The next visitor was Sergeant Witherspoon.

'Sit down, Sergeant,' Walsh offered, indicating a spare chair with a sweep of his hand. 'I understand you went out on some strange cases yesterday afternoon. Would you tell me about them? What made them so unusual?'

'Well, sir, it was like this,' Witherspoon replied, curious at having been called in so early in the morning to talk about a minor series of robberies to someone like Walsh, who he knew was concerned with an important murder inquiry. He couldn't for the life of him see how all this fitted in. 'Well, there were these four small country shops, you see, and each one had all the paper money taken from their tills, early yesterday afternoon. One of them was a post office as well as being a general store. At Coton that was. What was so strange was that in each case they swore blind that the shops had not been left unattended, not even for a moment. Yet one minute the money was there, and the next moment, it was gone. They all said that there was no way it could have happened, yet it had, if you follow my meaning. I took statements, of course, but there was nothing to follow up. What could I do, sir? The only logical explanation was the invisible man.' Sergeant Withersoon held both hands out in a gesture of helplessness. He couldn't see that he'd missed anything obvious, but was more than a little apprehensive in case he had.

'Hay's Butchers was one, as well as the general store at Coton. That right?' asked Walsh.

The sergeant nodded.

'Have a look through those cheques. Are they all from your four shops?' Walsh asked, pushing the small pile across the desk.

Witherspoon had a surprised look on his face as he carefully turned each one over.

'You're right, sir. They're all from those four shops I was at yesterday. Where on earth did they come from?' he asked.

'They were found in the room of a young man whose death we're investigating. I think it might be as well if you followed this up, because you're already involved. Come back at six and I'll brief you with the others. Then you'll know what's going on.'

At quarter to six, Detective Sergeant Reginald Finch appeared, all smiles, having driven straight from his course to Cambridge.

'What's the panic, boss? Hello, Brenda, how are you?' he greeted them, as he came in.

'Hello, Reg. Sorry to have pulled you off your course, but we've got a couple of murders on our hands. Come and sit in on this briefing, then I want you to take on the report vetting for me. There's so much paper coming at me at the moment, and there'll be even more soon. I can't keep on top of it by myself.' Walsh started to gather the files together.

'OK, boss, no problem,' replied Finch.

8

Walsh pushed open the double swing doors of the briefing room with his shoulder, and strode in.

The room was longer than it was wide, with browny–green curtains that had been drawn across the windows. Two tables stood together, end on, in front of which were thirteen or fourteen tubular steel chairs with blue moulded plastic seats.

Walsh sat down at one of the tables and set out his files in front of him. He looked up when the noise had ceased. Eight or nine people watched him expectantly.

He cleared his throat. 'Good morning,' he said, to start the proceedings. There was the usual silly business regarding the seating. 'Move in closer, then I don't have to shout,' he asked them irritably.

There was a general stirring as some of them moved to sit on the chairs directly in front of the table.

'We're investigating two murders now,' he announced. 'The first was Professor Higgins, killed in his study at home, between eight and eleven o'clock, two nights ago, by blows to the back of the head, probably using a short length of lead piping. It's likely that, when he returned from taking the dog for a walk, he disturbed an intruder. Therefore it's possible that his death was not intentional; however, that remains to be seen. Higgins was a very wealthy man, very wealthy. So money is a strong possible motive, and we still need to eliminate some possible suspects. Firstly, his wife. She went out that night to a charity reception and didn't get back home until three o'clock in the morning; but she left that reception early, possibly with sufficient time to kill her husband before going off somewhere else. Her story is that she'd had too much to drink, and drove out towards Royston, where she parked, and went to sleep. She doesn't remember where that was, or what time she left the party. I don't believe her, but that's your task, Walters. I want to know where she went, what she did, who she was with and why she doesn't want us to know.'

He looked at the young detective sergeant in front of him and handed over one of the files.

'That contains photos of her car, herself and the details of the other guests at the party. I don't want you to talk to her if you can avoid it, she's become hostile. So do your best with what I've given you. Do the local hotels, restaurants and clubs first.'

Walters screwed up his mouth slightly as he took the file. He didn't think much of this assignment: it had all the hallmarks of looking for a needle in a haystack.

'Higgins left a will, with a number of bequests to various people. Any one of those could be a suspect,' Walsh went on. 'That's your job, Myson. There's a list of people I want you to see, and a copy of the will. Find out where each was when Higgins and Varney were killed, and verify their stories as well. OK?' he inquired, eyebrows raised.

Myson nodded.

'Good. Now in that will the residue of his estate goes to his son, who lives in Royston. We've already had one statement from him and his wife, Robinson, but I want you to see them and find out where they were when Varney was killed, and check their stories thoroughly. Do it carefully. Nearly half a million makes for a very healthy motive.'

70

There was a murmur of surprise as they became aware just how wealthy Higgins had been.

'Another of the beneficiaries was a woman hypnotist, who Higgins had consulted in connection with a special project he was working on. On the night of the murder, she had several clients. I want them talked to, and her story for both occasions checked out thoroughly too. It doesn't take a big team to do that. You can handle that one, White, but in addition, I want you to find out if Varney had ever been one of her clients. He'd recently given up smoking.' He handed out another of the files. 'Lastly, on the Higgins case, I have a list of his students and a few others of the college staff. I hope you like going round the colleges, Jones, because that's what I want you to do. Here's the list. Find out all they know and where they were.'

Walsh paused, rubbed his chin, and picked his next words carefully. 'Higgins was a bit of an inventor, and he was working on a project that comes under a secrecy category. Some parts of that invention are missing. In fact, that's all we know for certain that is missing from his home, so it's important for us to know all those who had any idea of what he was doing. At some stage direct your questions around this point, and see what reaction you get, all right? That goes for all of you.' He paused, and moved some of the files about on the desk.

'Now we come to the death of George Varney. He was a young man of about twenty-five, who lived on his own in a one-bedroomed flat. One of three in a converted Victorian semi. He died during the evening before last, by having the right temple of his skull crushed in from a blow with a bottle of wine. We've done some calling on neighbours, but not enough. Thomas, I want you to follow up the house-to-house interviews. Find out all that his neighbours know about him, particularly concerning his visitors, and of course, the vehicles they drove.' He looked up and saw Thomas's cheerful face nodding thoughtfully. 'In the flat were a few postcards, and letters from various people. Here are photocopies, Howard. Find out who they are, how they are related, and what they can tell us about him.' Walsh paused again for a moment, cleared his throat, then carried on with the briefing. 'Right then. Varney is connected with the Higgins case, because he was one of the laboratory assistants who had helped Higgins with his project. Constable Phipps, here, went round to interview him in this connection and found him murdered. Now, here is a strange twist in the story. In Varney's flat we found some cheques and postal orders from a series of small robberies. They were carried out during the afternoon of the day that he died, in the villages to the south of the city, but we found none of the stolen money. Only Varney appears to have left prints on them after they were put in the tills. I need to know whether Varney did those jobs on his own, or if he had an accomplice with him. Sergeant Witherspoon has already started investigating, so he gets this one. Here are photos of Varney, Sergeant, and some photos of his moped and his riding gear. Someone must have seen him on his journey. You know now where he started and where he finished. In addition, we have a photo of someone else on a moped. It may be important, it may not, but find out who it is, right?'

He leaned back in his chair. 'Are there any questions?' He looked round at the faces in front of him, all busy turning over the documents in their respective files, all except Richard Packstone, who stared dreamily into space, lost in his own thoughts.

'Yes, sir,' Eric Walters said. 'This Mrs Higgins, did she have any boyfriends? There's nothing here in the files you gave me.'

'That's because we don't know of any, Eric. In your file there's copies of the opinions we've had so far. Certainly the relationship with her husband was not good. They disagreed over the treatment of their son, who sounds as though he's a lazy scrounger, but being brought up by a pair like that, there may be some justification. The general opinion appears to be that no one would have been surprised if she had got a boyfriend, but, as I say, there's no evidence that she has. From your point of view, it's unlikely that she spent all the time from half nine in the evening until three in the morning in bed with a lover. She could have spent much of that time in a public place, a bar or a restaurant for instance. You've got your work cut out to find just where she went, I appreciate that.'

Walsh raised his eyebrows, inquiring whether the question had been adequately answered. Apparently it had, for he received an affirmative nod.

'This hypnotist woman, sir. Is it in your mind that she might have influenced Higgins, put him in a trance and fixed his mind so that he would leave her money in his will, while at the same time she was planning to kill him?' asked Alan White.

'I don't know enough about hypnotism. Maybe that's possible, but I don't like coincidences,' Walsh replied.

Witherspoon then surprised him by asking the questions that they were all obviously curious about, but hadn't asked. 'Sir!' Witherspoon said. 'About these robberies. No one saw him in the shops. Why do you think anyone would have seen him coming or going?'

Walsh looked at him thoughtfully. 'I don't think that you'll find he was invisible. Higgins's secret project was concerned with the subconcious mind, but I don't want that talked about. It is quite conceivable that Higgins's stolen invention was used in those robberies to blank out the memories of those people in the shops. That's all I can tell you about it,' Walsh replied. 'Any more questions just now? OK, then, you've got a few minutes before you talk to your teams. I'll be back here in the office at nine, if you need me. Get your routine reports in as quickly as possible or phone in if you find out anything you think is important.

Contact either myself, Brenda Phipps or Reg Finch, who will be based in the office for the next few days. Good luck, then.'

He gathered the remaining files from the table, and went back to his office.

'I'm going home for a shave and a bath. I'll see you both later,' he told his two assistants.

At home Walsh lay soaking in the bath and tried hard to blank out the confusion of thoughts that still raced through his mind. He succeeded very well, and dropped off to sleep. Gwen woke him later by splashing water over his face.

'Come on, Nudie, I've got a meal ready downstairs, and the sight of you there's giving me funny feelings,' she said huskily.

Walsh made a grab for her, but she eluded him with ease.

'Naughty, naughty, don't get randy,' she laughed as she went back downstairs.

Walsh sat down at the table feeling much refreshed.

'I've brought Reg Finch back off his course for a few days, while the pressure's on,' he told Gwen.

'Now that's nice. How is he? Let's have him and Margaret round for dinner before he goes back. I'd like that,' she replied. 'You could invite Brenda as well. Has she got a boyfriend?'

Walsh confessed that he didn't know.

'Well, never mind. How about Sunday evening? Let me know, will you? I'll need to get some shopping done.'

Walsh grinned. Gwen loved putting on a dinner.

It was after half-past nine by the time he got back to his office. Both Brenda and Reginald Finch were in there, working.

74

'You don't mind us working in here, do you, boss?' Finch replied. 'Someone's using my old office.'

'No problem.' He left them to it and went along to the C.C.'s office.

'I'm not at all happy about this damned machine of Higgins's, sir,' he said, frowning. 'From the sound of it you can walk in, switch it on, and do what the devil you like. Nobody even knows that you've been there. What's worrying me is what we do when we find the person who's got it. We're just as vulnerable as anyone else, and could get the same treatment. I know we're not in that position yet, but when we are, I want some protection for our people, and for me as well. I suppose you realize that with that thing, someone could even wander about in Headquarters here.' He rubbed his left ear anxiously. 'Do you recall Joe Mason? He retired about three years back, because he was going deaf. I wouldn't mind having him hanging about, down in reception. Higgins's machine shouldn't affect him if he switches his hearing aid off, and he'd be useful when we close in on the killer. What do you think?'

'You know, you've got a point there, Sidney. I hadn't considered it myself, but your suggestion sounds practical. Do that, and get some more deaf people, if you can find them. You can work them on shifts, if that'll put your mind at rest. It might also pay us to contact that government department. You still need clarification of the data in Higgins's computer; let them find us an expert to advise us, one that meets with their security requirements. In any case, they're sure to have been working on the protective angle,' the C.C. suggested.

So it was that ex-Sergeant Joe Mason returned to duty, on a temporary basis. He'd been a judo expert and was a useful man to have around. Walsh was pleased to see him looking fit and well. He wasn't told the true reason for his assistance being required, but it wouldn't have mattered if there'd been no explanation at all. He was delighted to break the monotonous routine of his life. He could lip read perfectly well and with his massive hearing aid he could hear conversation, and the classical music that had become such an important part of his life. He was quite happy to file patrol reports in the front office next to the reception area.

It was a dry, warm morning. A light breeze swirled the first fallen leaves of autumn on the bare patches under the trees near the Engineering Laboratory.

'A doubly unhappy situation, coming so soon after the death of the Professor. I don't know what the world is coming to, I really don't. Poor Mrs Higgins, what a terrible loss,' the lab director exclaimed. His face was pale, lined with stress, and his interlocked fingers twitched nervously.

'You knew her well, did you?' Walsh asked.

'Not that well, but I often met her at charity functions. We like to be involved in such things here, it helps maintain cordial relations between the University and the town, you see.'

'You didn't attend the reception at Councillor Stevens' the other night,' Brenda pointed out bluntly.

'That's true, I didn't, but I had someone deputize for me. I had other things to do, we played bridge with my sister-in-law and her husband, if I remember correctly.'

'Varney and someone else worked with Professor Higgins quite recently, I believe. You must have known about that, I should imagine?' Walsh inquired.

'Of course, but it was a relatively minor project. Some micro-chip circuits in an experimental audio sound projector. I wasn't interested in the details. It wasn't a University matter, you see, but something to do with the Professor's private hobby. You're not suggesting that that had anything to do with his death, and that of young Varney, surely? I wouldn't have thought that was likely, but you know your own business best.'

'Would you tell us about your security arrangements? Obviously some of the work you do here must have a secrecy classification. What checks do you do on your staff?' Walsh asked.

The director looked embarrassed. 'You must bear in mind that we are primarily a teaching laboratory. The research we undertake cannot seriously be classified as top secret, so we have no more than a general security vetting. That's undertaken by our personnel staff. We're a little loath to encroach on the political affinities of individuals.'

'This is where George Varney worked, Inspector.'

Walsh spent a few moments studying the face of the short, dark-haired woman in the white overall. There was a regular prettiness about the features and the bone structure was good, but the effect of the challenging, dark, steady eyes was disconcerting.

'My section's upstairs. I'm only standing in as supervisor because Briggs is off sick, you understand,' she continued.

Walsh nodded and looked round the laboratory.

There were oscilloscopes, meters and banks of equipment with all sorts of dials and switches on the benches.

Walsh pulled open a drawer. It contained some pencils, a notepad full of figures and calculations, a tabloid newspaper folded open at a half-finished crossword, and a chocolate bar.

'He was working on this model "linear motion" demonstrator,' Miss Laurelen added, pointing to a contraption of rods and coils of wire. 'Not much more to do, from the look of it. That's one of the educational equipment projects.'

'You know all the different projects they're working on, do you?' Brenda asked.

'In my section, yes, of course I do. I'm responsible for planning work-loads, as well as discipline, safety and that sort of thing, so I have to know. Down here, I'm only concerned whether they're working to the timetable. Briggs'll be back next week, I hope. He's the man in charge of this section.'

'Some weeks ago Professor Higgins had the use of two of these people. What was all that about?' Walsh inquired.

'Briggs was here then. I don't know what they were up to.'

'What aspect of engineering do you specialize in?' Brenda asked politely.

'I'm concerned with chemical engineering and computer programming,' Laurelen replied bluntly.

'How well did you know Varney?' asked Walsh.

'Socially, you mean? Not at all. I know nothing about his private life, and little enough about him here. He didn't have the same interests as me, or else I would have met him at the places I go to, but don't ask me what his interests were, I couldn't tell you. I think he was a quiet young man, happy enough with his own company, but I don't really know, I'm afraid.'

'But don't you have dinners and dances, at Christmas and so on?' Walsh persisted.

'Yes, of course we do, but there's an awful lot of people work for the University, you know. I don't actually remember ever seeing him at one. He might have gone to them, I don't know.'

'Can you remember what you did during the evening, three nights back, and also the night before last?' Walsh asked.

Laurelen paused, thinking. 'I went to a meeting at the Blackfriars Hall, the first night, that was on the need for social change, but the night before last, I was at home on my own, I'm afraid.'

'Do you have a car, Miss Laurelen, or a moped perhaps?' Brenda asked.

'I've a Fiesta, it's two years old, and red. My bra's a 32B, and I've got white knickers on, or they were when I got dressed this morning. Anything else you want to know?'

'How long have you been personnel officer, Mr Harrison?' Walsh asked, leaning his elbows on the table in the small office the lab director had found for them to use.

The short, tubby, middle-aged man with the thinning fair hair hesitated for a moment. 'About fifteen years or thereabouts. Now, here is George Varney's file. He came to us straight from school at the age of eighteen, with three A levels. Quite a bright boy, really. Then he studied at the Technical College and got his ONCs and HNCs. Yes, he'd done very well. He had no home life, poor fellow; his father went off when he was very young, then his mother died. So he lived with his grandfather after that. When he could afford it, he got himself a bedsit, then later on, a flat. I see here that I gave him a reference at that time. Not much else, only assessment reviews. Social activities are noted as satisfactory. That doesn't tell us a lot, does it? I'm afraid I can't tell you much from a personal point of view. We do organize a lot of social events, and they are always well attended, but whether he went to them, I can't tell you. I wouldn't know his particular friends. His workmates and Miss Laurelen will probably be able to help you there,' he suggested.

'Miss Laurelen wasn't able to help us much. She says she knows nothing about his private life,' Brenda said.

'Oh really! Is that so?' he replied hesitantly. 'Well, it takes all types to make the world, doesn't it? These are the record files of all the people that work on this floor. They're the ones most likely to be able to help you.'

'Before we get down to those, did Varney have a clothes locker? If he did, then I'd like to take a look inside,' Walsh interrupted.

'Yes, certainly he did. I should have thought of that myself. I keep all the master keys in my office safe, I'll go and get the duplicates for you,' Harrison replied and hurried away.

'You've already seen one of these people, haven't you, Brenda?'

'That's right. What was his name now?' she replied, brushing the wayward lock of hair from her brow. 'Holmes, I think. Have you got a Holmes file there?'

Walsh nodded, and opened it. 'We'll start with him, then, when we've looked at Varney's locker.'

The lockers were in a cloakroom, just down the corridor. Harrison took hold of the padlock, turning it so that he could see the keyhole. As he pulled at it, it clicked and came open. 'That's not much good, is it?' he muttered. 'Anyway, there it is. It's open now.' He moved back, out of the way.

Walsh pulled the door wide. It contained two white overalls, a pair of shoes, a raincoat and some technical magazines. There was nothing in any of the pockets. He turned his attention to the broken padlock. He pushed the clasp in; it clicked, but the levers were broken, and he could pull it open again with very little effort. There was a faint mark under the clasp. It could have been levered open but it was difficult to be sure. He tried the locks on several of the other doors nearby; two pulled open in just the same way. He looked at Harrison and shrugged his shoulders. 'Your folk don't seem particularly concerned about their own security, do they?'

Holmes was a thin, sandy-haired man in his middle thirties. A wispy moustache covered the upper lip of the pale drawn, hollow-cheeked face, out of which peered lustre-less blue eyes.

'I'm very sorry to hear about poor George. He wasn't a bad chap. I can't understand why anyone should want to do him any harm. He hadn't got any enemies, he wasn't that kind of bloke. He never had much luck but he kept going like we all have to do, trying to maintain a decent way of life on a pittance, in the midst of all the luxury and sloth of the establishment. His dad was a no-good, and his poor old mum wore herself out trying to bring him up right. Then he had to live with his sour old grandfather. So the poor sod grew up always expecting the worst, but he tried to make something of himself, and got away from the old man as soon as he could. He was so pleased when he got his flat. "I've got peace when I shut my front door on the rest of the world," is what he once said to me. He wasn't bitter, though, he'd do anything for anybody, but you'd have to ask first, he was so shy. Even me, and I've known him since he came to work here. If I didn't speak to him first, he'd sit there and say nothing, all day long if need be. Yes, he must have been lonely, but what chance did he have? He hadn't got anything, and with his upbringing, he'd got no social graces, so he had no friends. I was probably his best mate, but we never went anywhere together. I've got a wife and two kids, haven't I? So I couldn't, could I? He used to go to the social club do's, if there was anything special on, but I never saw him dance or try to chat up any girls. Though you could see he wanted to. He'd watch them, but he couldn't pluck up the courage, now the poor sod never will.' Holmes rubbed at the corner of one eye with a finger, the nail of which wasn't particularly clean.

'I'd better go to his funeral. If I don't there'll be no bugger there for the poor sod,' he muttered. 'Did he smoke, you ask. Well, yes, he used to, until quite recently. Then he gave it up. "Robin," he said to me, "it's a waste of money. If I can kick the habit I'll save a fortune," but he didn't find it

82

easy. Eventually he went to one of those hypnotists, out Sawston way. It seemed to do the trick, even though I'd told him he was throwing good money after bad.'

'How did he get on with his supervisor? Was he happy in his work?' Brenda asked.

'We all get on with Briggs OK. I hope he comes back soon. This Laurelen bitch,' Holmes continued with a sneer, 'she's too high and bloody mighty even to sit at our table in the canteen, for all her talk of human rights. She's a knocker-down, she is, with nothing to put in its place. Even I'm not that stupid. Was he happy? Well, I suppose he was, in his way. He'd got a job doing what he liked doing, that's something, I suppose. Where was I on the nights Higgins and Varney died? At home with the wife and kids, that's where. I don't get no chance to go mogging off on me own, do I? But if there's any way I can help you, don't you hesitate to ask. I'd like to get my hands on the bastard that did the poor bugger in.' The muscles of his jaw tightened and the long slender fingers of his hands clenched until the knuckles grew white. His blue eyes hardened and glinted with the strength of his anger.

Walsh thanked him, and asked him to send in another member of the staff.

There were over a dozen other files, names to be transposed into the faces of real people, probing questions to be asked and answers noted. Eventually Walsh stood up and stretched his cramped limbs. 'Thank goodness for that,' he said. 'We might have been wasting our time, but it had to be done.'

They gave the personnel files back to Harrison and walked back to Headquarters. The sky had become heavily overcast, and they increased their pace as a faint drizzle started to fall.

'There's been a visitor called to see you, sir. Wouldn't

give a name, said he'd come as a result of your London telephone call. Said he'd call back at five, sir,' the duty sergeant informed him.

'Let me know when he comes. I'll be in my office,' Walsh replied.

'It's good of you to see me, Mr Briggs. I understand you've been in hospital, having an operation. I hope you're feeling much better,' Brenda said sympathetically to the grey-haired, hollow-cheeked man, slumped listlessly in the easy chair opposite.

'I can't say I do feel much better. They mess you about so much in that place, you can't get any sleep. There's too much going on all the time, and when you do doze off, blow me if they don't come along to take your temperature, give you some pills or turn you over. They're ever so good, really, I suppose, but I'm damned glad to be back home, I can tell you. Now, what was it you wanted to talk to me about? The wife said it was to do with young Varney. What's he been up to? Isn't like him to get into trouble.'

'Oh dear, you don't know then. I'm sorry to have to tell you that George Varney was found dead in his flat, a couple of nights ago. He'd been killed by a blow to the head. We're trying to find out about his private life. That's why I've come to see you,' Brenda replied.

Briggs looked shocked. 'Oh Lord, that's awful. Poor chap. Why on earth would anyone do a thing like that? Was it robbery? I can't imagine he'd got much worth pinching.'

'Nothing appears to have been stolen, Mr Briggs. We think he'd either had a quarrel with a friend or that it's somehow linked with Professor Higgins's death. You knew about that, I suppose?'

Briggs nodded, then shook his head. 'I don't know if I can be of much help to you, really. George made up some circuit panels for the Professor, a week or two before I went

84

into hospital. If I remember right, young Robin Holmes was on that as well. I think he did the "speakers". I wouldn't have thought that had a lot to do with it, though. Hardly worth killing people for that sort of thing. As to George's friends, I can't say I've met any, in fact I don't think he had any. Quiet sort of fellow, shy like, if you know what I mean. Not exactly one for the girls, but you never know with these young fellows these days, what they'll get up to. He really needed a nice girl to help him settle down. No, he was a good worker, I never had any trouble from him, and he was keen to learn, specially the latest developments. I'm going to miss it all, you know,' he admitted regretfully. 'I'm getting too old, and this trouble of mine's taken a lot out of me. Another year, and then I'll take early retirement. No problem there, they want to rationalize the administration, so they'll merge my department with the one upstairs then. Yes, that young woman will take it over. A clever girl, broken home, you know; has her silly ways, but she works hard. Still, we all mellow as we get older, don't we?'

10

Walsh's visitor was a tall, thin man of about forty, dressed in a light brown suit.

'My name's Hutchinson. I'm the adviser that you asked for, on the late Professor Higgins's work, that is,' he said as an introduction, his keen bright eyes watching Walsh with interest.

'Any official identification documents?' Walsh asked politely.

Hutchinson shook his head.

Walsh looked at him thoughtfully. There was a point being made here, a challenge even. He reached out for the phone and dialled the London number. 'I have a visitor, re Professor Higgins. He's six foot two, slim build, approximately twelve stone, light brown hair with left parting, receding, has small mole just below the right ear and a split right thumb nail. Can you confirm that this is your man? Calls himself "Hutchinson", by the way.' Walsh stared at the wall, avoiding the gaze of his visitor, while this was being considered, in some office, somewhere in London. The reply was affirmative.

'They say I can trust you with the Crown Jewels. I don't happen to have them on me at the moment,' he announced humorously.

'Never mind, I'm glad you did that. It makes me a little more comfortable, surprisingly enough. Tell me how I can help you, then I'll tell you what you can do for me.'

'This damned gadget of Higgins's is giving me the willies. Here we are trying to find a double murderer, and if we catch up with him, all he needs to do is press a switch and our minds go blotto, so to speak. What I'd like from you is a full understanding of the effects of the thing, and then what measures can be taken against it,' Walsh explained.

'Yes, I can understand your concern, but tell me, you said "a double murderer". I'm only aware of the death of Higgins.'

Walsh's mouth pulled tight in the corners. He suddenly felt guilty, as though Varney's death was his own fault.

'We went to talk to one of the lab assistants that helped Higgins build the machine, and found him dead in his bed, with his head bashed in,' Walsh admitted bluntly.

'Oh dear! That must have been a bit of a shock,' Hutchinson murmured sympathetically.

'But that wasn't all,' Walsh continued. 'In the man's flat we found a number of cheques stolen that afternoon in four small robberies, just out of town, and in each of those robberies the people neither saw nor heard a thing. I think Higgins's machine was used. It's possible that the lab assistant killed Higgins, took the machine, used it, then got killed by someone else. So tell me, do you think the machine could be used in the way I think it was?'

'The short answer is – most probably. Let me explain precisely what Higgins was up to. It was he himself who first suggested that it might be possible to simulate a variety of reactions in the mind, not only in humans but in animals and birds as well, by the use of certain sound sequences. You might say, of course, that the simple mimicking of natural cries such as mating calls and warning cries has been used for centuries; and you'd be right. What he believed was that this was evidence of a direct pathway into the subconscious section of the mind, the part that contains the inherited survival instincts. It contains the baby's instinct to suck at the nipple, for example, and a

87

young pigeon's knowledge of navigation and feather preening. He felt sure that there was, in humans, a "stay still and quiet" reaction to the right sounds, just as in the young of many other species. In other words, behaviour characteristics which were already programmed in the mind at birth. Anyway, it was considered, by certain parties, a piece of original research that was well worth encouraging, in the national interest, that is to say. It was felt that we had to do it, just in case someone else did, then we would be able to try and develop counter-measures. I might add that the general consensus of opinion was that it wasn't going to be practical; however, since the cost was minimal, it went ahead. Each week Higgins was to send us a full report on what he was doing. We made a mistake, though: we should have insisted that he worked in a properly secure laboratory. But before we knew it, he was working on the voices of hypnotists, without giving us a chance to check them out from the security point of view. That really threw the cat amongst the pigeons, but it also caused the committee to reassess his chances of success to over fifty per cent; so up went the security rating of the project. Then, without telling us, he had his prototype made, up here, in the Marlborough Teaching Laboratories. Barmy bloke, Higgins,' Hutchinson said, tapping his fingers lightly on Walsh's desk.

'Even so,' he continued, 'I think he was surprised at the effectiveness of his experiments. He tested it on one of the lab assistants at a range of about eight or ten feet, and it worked just as he had planned. The chap's mind blanked and he stayed quite still, for about seven or eight minutes, but Higgins frightened himself when he calculated what the effects might have been if the volume had been set higher. According to him, having penetrated into the subconscious, too high a volume would do harm, permanently, to the operation of the mind and its ability, in consciousness, to reason logically. In other words, it could make someone completely mad. He was so concerned about this that he made some alterations to his circuits to ensure that if the volume was turned up, the length of time the sound burst was transmitted was reduced to compensate. That was a safety measure he considered necessary, even on his experimental model. However, although his initial success was unexpected, the committee's pessimistic opinions weren't really so far wrong. Since he was so frightened to use high volumes, it was going to be virtually impossible to increase the effective range of the instrument. Still a very useful gadget but not what he was hoping he would achieve.'

He saw Walsh's eyebrows rise slightly, and correctly interpreted the question. 'Yes! We wanted Higgins to end up with a machine that could take control of riot situations, football matches, that sort of thing, but it would have been very useful in many other ways. Well, that's what Higgins was up to. Now, I must remove from Cambridge all the notes Higgins made, and the details of his computer model. It's much too dangerous to leave lying about. Then it's up to you to recover the missing prototype.'

'There may well be a missing copy of the computer program as well,' Walsh told him. 'If we've reconstructed the circumstances of Higgins's death correctly, he was looking at his computer screen when he was struck down. He could only just have returned from walking his dog, you see, so that suggests the intruder was operating it. I gather there's a thing called a tape streamer, that copies very quickly. Trouble is, in this town, there's a hell of a lot of people that do know what they're doing with computers. Be that as it may, tell me how we can protect ourselves from the effects of the machine. That's what concerns me most at the moment.'

'It's not as straightforward as that. Of course we've made up our own duplicate of the prototype, for testing purposes. We've tried proprietary ear-plugs, earphones, and the kind of helmets your men on motor bikes wear, but they're not designed to completely cut out all sounds, only to reduce the decibel level to an acceptable one, or, as in the case of your motor cyclists, enough for them to hear their radios. So we've had to look at other things. The simplest and most effective we've found is a sort of plastic bag over the head, inflated with air. The trouble with that is, unless you've got some form of breathing apparatus, you'll suffocate yourself eventually. It's got to be some kind of space helmet, really,' Hutchinson replied.

'Is that all you can come up with? I can't have members of my force walking around with plastic bags over their heads, or glass domes either; we'd be a laughing stock. I've brought in one of our ex-policemen who was retired early, because of increasing deafness. What about that? Is that likely to be any good?' Walsh asked.

'Well done! Human deafness. To be honest, you've probably hit on the only sure way to combat the danger, provided he is properly deaf, not just partially.'

'Thank goodness for that. I'll see if I can round up some more, then. What about jamming the sounds, like the Russians did to radio broadcasts?' suggested Walsh.

'It's difficult to do that effectively. Higgins's machine uses pulses of varying frequencies, you see, beamed forward, so that the user is unaffected. We found that the intensity of a jamming signal necessary to blot out the Higgins sounds, played continuously, since you don't know when a Higgins pulse will hit you, would drive you all nutty anyway,' Hutchinson commented ruefully.

'There is one other thing,' Walsh remarked, his own fingers now tapping impatiently on the desk. 'I understand it only affects ninety-eight people out of a hundred. Is that true? Is there any way of finding the odd two per cent?'

'That's very interesting too. That's the percentage of people who can't be hypnotized. We think such people might have some defect in the inner ear, or their hereditary instinct modes are faulty in some way. It might be so. You'd have to test a lot of people to find out,' Hutchinson replied.

'Will you arrange for all the people in this force to be tested, then?' Walsh demanded positively.

'I like you, Inspector. You really get your teeth into something and hang on, don't you? I suppose it can be arranged. Out of courtesy I ought to check with the top dogs, but take it from me, we'll do it, if it'll make you feel happier. It can be part of our testing programme. I must warn you again of the point I've already made about the effect of the volume control. If someone's copied Higgins's computer data, as you think, and that person knows his way about computer programs, he could bypass that safety circuit Higgins built in, then with the full volume in operation, you could really be up against a dangerous machine.'

Walsh scowled, and stuck doggedly to his guns. Hutchinson's attitude seemed far too philosophical for his liking. 'Would you like to use my phone to make your courtesy call to the top dogs? Then perhaps we can get this testing set up.'

The first testing was arranged to take place during the ten o'clock briefing that night, when the patrols changed over.

The duty sergeant looked bewildered when told to organize three further meetings during the next twelve hours, to include the whole of the rest of the force, uniformed and plain-clothed, at all levels. This, on top of the introduction of a deaf assistant in his office.

He shrugged it off, in the sure knowledge that he was the only sane one in the whole place, and that there was never much sense in many of the instructions he was required to carry out, anyway.

Walsh drove Hutchinson out to Higgins's house and unlocked the study door.

The computer was switched on.

91

'He doesn't appear to have changed anything here since he sent in his last progress report, but I'll run another copy, to be on the safe side, then I'll wipe out the memories off the hard disc. It'll be quite clean then,' Hutchinson remarked, after a considerable period of time.

Walsh gave a tired grunt in reply, and sat down to wait in the Professor's old leather armchair, the one with the bright, flower-embroidered cushion.

It was nice to have five minutes' peace, just to sit and think.

Was Marion Dubonnet involved in these killings? It was difficult to imagine anything sinister behind those wonderfully deep blue eyes. He could visualize them so clearly that it made his head swim, just as it had when he'd been with her. It was an effort to force his mind to think of other things.

For what purpose had Higgins's hypnotizing machine been stolen? He tried to put aside, for the moment, the possibility that it was taken as a blind, deliberately to put him on the wrong track, for he desperately wanted to hang on to motives he knew and could understand. Higgins's wealth, his son's need for money, Mrs Higgins having a lover, or even jealousy of the man's intellectual achievements. Varney's killing detracted somewhat from all those motives, slightly but not completely. Varney could easily have been an accomplice of the murderer; just as easily he could have been the murderer himself. If that was the case, then his motive must have been personal gain, to use the machine for petty robbery, unless, of course, he'd found a buyer. A buyer who'd killed him instead of paying hard cash, or maybe to eliminate the possibility of Varney subsequently blackmailing him. That someone might have set the whole thing up in the first place. It could be one of the Higgins family, who had met Varney when he had visited Higgins at his home, or someone else at the lab, or someone unknown; the girl on the moped perhaps. What about a foreign espionage agent? That would fit in just as well, but in that case Varney must have tried a double-cross, or else he wouldn't have been killed, or would he? After all, there was no sign of a fight, or of the flat being thoroughly searched by a professional, but the possibility remained. He must remember to talk to Hutchinson about foreign agents before he left. His mind had travelled a full circle, back to what use was to be made of the machine. Was it for use in robberies, or for its international potential as an embryo military weapon? His mind was going round and round, unable to settle to serious thought, almost as though it was no longer part of his material body, a body which now lay limp and useless in the chair, and those deep blue Dubonnet eyes still drew him into their unfathomable, confusing depths.

Hutchinson shook him by the shoulder. 'Come on, old chap. Wakey wakey, rise and shine. I've finished here now,' he said, smiling down with all the complacency of someone who hadn't missed a full night's sleep.

'Just resting my eyelids,' growled Walsh hoarsely, as he struggled to stand up. 'By the way, have your chaps found anything that might suggest that this is all caused by some foreign power?' he continued hopefully.

'Not a thing. In fact the consensus of opinion is that it's a civil matter, but we haven't given up yet, I can assure you. We've checked out the most obvious agents and are now left with those that might, but probably didn't. If I make myself clear,' Hutchinson replied.

'You do. Thanks a lot.'

'Well, come on then, we've still a lot of work to do,' Hutchinson replied.

'Git lost. Yer must be bloody joking,' the burly young man sitting astride the powerful, black Harley Davidson motor bike replied. 'What the hell makes you think we'd help the likes of you?'

'You'd like the bloke that spied on you caught, wouldn't you?' Brenda asked, casually running her fingers over the shining chrome of the high handlebars.

'Maybe, if we caught him, not you. He wouldn't do it again in a hurry, or lots of other things, likely.'

A slim, black-leather-clad youngster, who was standing nearby listening, giggled. 'Yeah,' was his contribution to the conversation.

'So there's no way you'll help us catch this prowler then?'

The burly boy grinned, and eyed her up and down appreciatively. 'Didn't say that, did I? We only do favours for them that's in our group, so's if you'd like to join you're welcome. I wouldn't mind having you across the back of me bike, even if you are a bloody rozzer.'

'Or she could fight you and become the leader; we ain't had a woman one before,' the slim boy chipped in, still giggling.

'Shut up, you,' the burly one snapped. 'He's right, though, you could fight me for it.'

'We're trained in self-defence, you know,' Brenda said, looking at him thoughtfully.

'We know a thing or two ourselves,' he replied, a little surprised, but giving back stare for stare.

'How's the winner decided?'

'Simple, the loser cries off, if he's still alive. Loud enough so's everyone can hear, but there ain't no other rules, anything goes,' he warned

'Where do we fight? Here?'

'You ain't bloody serious, are you? You're only a skinny bitch. Yer wouldn't stand a chance,' he said incredulously.

Brenda's pretty face creased into a lovely smile. 'You're not scared, are you?'

'Me scared? Like hell, you stupid bitch. Well, if you want a thrashing, you'll get one. Here'll do, as well as anywhere.'

'Just a minute, then.' Brenda's hand reached up to

remove the tiny gold studs from her ears, and she un-strapped her wrist-watch. She walked over to the car.

'Look after these for me, please,' she asked Sergeant Smith who sat watching from the driver's seat.

'I couldn't hear. What the hell are you up to, Brenda?'

'Nothing to worry about. He just wants a demonstration of self-defence, then he'll help us. It'd be better if you stayed here. I can handle it.'

Smith knew of Brenda's reputation in both defence and attack, but he protested, nevertheless. 'You're a stupid bugger, Brenda. Don't you know the first rule in the force is not to take any risks? For Christ's sake, girl, you'll get us both into a load of trouble,' Smith protested.

'I'm not taking any risks, don't worry.'

'He'll go for your hair, girl, watch out for dirty tricks,' he called anxiously after her.

The burly boy had taken off his jacket. His arms rippled with hard muscle.

The two contestants faced each other in conventional film-set attitudes, hunched forward, warily circling, watching for the other's first move.

He made the first, but he didn't go for her hair. It was a rapid, straight-fingered, straight left-arm thrust, for the pit of her stomach, while his right fist swung towards her face to distract her.

Brenda turned in a flash, sideways and back, catching his outstretched fingers with her left hand, his left wrist with her right, and twisted the arm inwards, pulling him forward and down. It's not as easy as it's made out for a light person to throw a heavy one, and Brenda didn't try. She back-kicked his legs away, so that he fell flat on his face, scrabbling to turn and relieve the pressure on his arm. He had no chance to do that, not after Brenda's right foot had come down hard on the back of his left shoulder, heel in the armpit, and she pulled the wrist up harder, forcing his face into the gravel.

95

'Give up?' she asked, rather breathlessly.

'Bastard!' was the reply through clenched teeth.

Brenda shrugged, twisted the wrist a bit more, and bent the fingers back as well.

The boy gave a muffled howl of pain.

'Want some more?' she asked.

'No! No! That's enough, you bloody bitch.'

'Come on, louder. So everyone can hear.'

'I give up, you effing bastard.'

Brenda let go, and jumped back, tense and alert. The leather-clad group round about eyed her maliciously. The burly boy struggled to his feet, clutching his painful shoulder.

'Right then, now we can sit down quietly, and work out how we're going to catch this prowler, can't we?' Brenda said confidently, defusing the tension.

The burly boy stood, angry, flushed and embarrassed, but he'd been given a way out with honour, and decided to play along.

'You were bloody lucky. If my bleeding foot hadn't slipped I'd've broken your flaming back. Just what is it you want us to do?'

'Somewhere or other someone learned your plans for the other night. I want you to set things up again, exactly the same as you did before. Go to the same places, at the same times, and talk as you did before. That way there's a chance the man we want will get to know about it.'

'You won't talk about this, will you Sarge?'

'No way. I'm not getting involved. In fact, I'm not even here. You're a crazy young kid, Brenda, but I hope it works out all right. You're a right goer, I'll say that for you,' Sergeant Smith said as he drove away from the car-park of the pub, half-way between Cambridge and Royston.

96

11

It was shortly before nine o'clock next morning, Saturday, when Walsh, instead of sitting at his desk, took the case files and the latest reports over to the little coffee table between the two low easy chairs that he used for informal interviews. He stretched himself out in one of them, and proceeded to read.

At about ten thirty, Brenda came in.

'We've got five all told, Chief, that's including me. Cheeky sod with the black box said he'd like to do further tests, but I've heard that one before,' she told him, indignation and humour combining to form a grin.

Walsh looked at her in bewilderment for a moment, then he recalled the tests with Higgins's machine.

'So you're Higgins-proof, are you? That's good. Who are the others? I'll arrange things so that they are based in the building, in shifts. With our deaf friends as well, we'll have at least two available at any moment of the day or night.'

'That'll add to the speculation. They all think you've flipped your lid, Chief, and that's putting it nicely,' Brenda informed him.

A smile came on to his face. 'It'll give them something to think about. Has Hutchinson's man gone now?'

'I think so. He wasn't too pleased about having to hang about here all night. Why? Did you want to see him? I'll check, if you want.'

'No, it doesn't matter. We've got plenty to do here.'

The telephone rang.

'There's an American major on the phone, sir. Wants to talk to the man in charge of the Higgins case. Shall I put him on?' the telephonist asked.

There was a click.

'Hello, Inspector Walsh here. I'm in charge of the investigation into the death of Professor Higgins. I understand you want to talk to me about it.'

'Hello there, Inspector. Yes, I do, but it's a little difficult. I'm not so sure that I'm not interfering. Anyhows, let me tell you that I've been speaking to Madge Higgins and she's mighty upset with you fellows.' He paused.

'Go on,' interrupted Walsh. 'It might be of help if I knew who I'm speaking to.'

'Well, that's just the problem, she doesn't want you to know. She says it's none of your business. You see, she was with me that night when the Professor was killed. Myself, I think she's got it all wrong, and so I told her. As sure as hell, you've got your teeth into her, and the longer she holds out the worse it'll get.'

'If she was with you, then I'd like a statement from you. As you say, it's the most sensible thing to do. Now, who are you and where are you?' Walsh demanded.

'Now, you look here, Inspector, I'm a serving US officer and if I don't want to talk, I won't.' He paused again. 'Oh, what the hell, I phoned you up to tell you anyway. I'm Major Douglas J. Hammond, and I'm at Mildenhall base right now, but I've got to go back to the States in thirty-six hours, and I've got lots to do before then. If you want to talk to me, and get your statement, you'd better do it soon.'

'Thank you, Major. I'll come over right away. Will you meet me at the main gate? It would be better, I think. I know your security is pretty tight,' Walsh replied cautiously.

'Sure is, Inspector. I'll meet you, and I'll buy you a drink

98

in the Mess. What's the time now? Can you get out here by twelve thirty, do you think? That OK with you?'

'Meet me at my car in two minutes Brenda,' Walsh said.

Once they were out of the city there was a fine dual carriageway to Newmarket.

'So, something's moving at last then, Chief,' Brenda remarked conversationally.

'Could be,' said Walsh bluntly, and concentrated on his driving.

Walsh was amused by the formality of the neat flower-beds, closely mown lawns and bright, white-painted kerb-stones, but tried not to glance towards the two very smart guards at the main gate, with their deadly hand-held automatic weapons, both of whom looked suspiciously in his direction. He always felt absurdly tense when there were firearms about: some basic instinct made him want to dive flat on the ground, and wriggle away into cover.

'We've come to see Major Hammond, he's expecting us,' he told the sergeant at the window in the guard house.

'He sure is. Just you come on in through that door.'

Major Hammond was a six-foot, broad-shouldered, fit-looking man in his fifties. The top part of his head was bald and sun-tanned and he wore an immaculate light brown uniform.

Walsh introduced himself and Brenda, showing his identity card.

'Delighted to meet you both. I'll just book you in and get you both passes, then I'll take you over to the Mess. We can talk there,' Hammond said, while shaking their hands effusively.

The Officers' Mess Bar was spacious and sumptuously furnished. They settled down on soft, deep, comfortable chairs at a table in one corner.

'Now, Inspector, let me start at the beginning. I knew

99

Madge Wright, as she was then, when we were both at college in Cambridge. We were sweethearts, you might say, for a while. We'd even made plans for the future together, but something broke us up. I can't even remember what it was, now, but that's not important. I'd nearly finished my exams there. Anyway, she got engaged to this guy Higgins and they got married a bit too quick, I thought. So I just got on with my own life, you understand, but I never could really forget her. Often I'd think about her and wonder what she was doing. I got married myself, and had a couple of kids, but last year my wife died, she'd had cancer for some time by then, and none of the treatment could stop it, so in the end I suppose it was the best thing.'

A white-jacketed waiter brought over a tray of drinks and put it down on the table in front of them. The Major took the opportunity of the interruption to blink back the moisture that had crept into his eyes.

Walsh looked away in polite embarrassment, but Brenda's eyes remained firmly on the speaker's face, watching his every expression.

Major Hammond took a long drink from his glass before he continued. 'Anyways, I came over a few weeks ago. I hadn't been back in England for several years, and I suppose I just got a bit nostalgic. I couldn't seem to shake off the memories that seemed to come flooding back, and I gave into them. It wasn't difficult to find her in the phone book, there aren't that many professors with that name. So I rang her, one afternoon. Well, we chatted a bit then I suggested that we might meet. I think she was a bit wary of that, but maybe she felt sorry for me. Me having lost my wife, and all that. Anyway we did meet, in Cambridge, and, I'm not kidding you, it just seemed as though all those years in between had never been. It was as though nothing had really changed. That's sure how it was for me, and I think she felt the same. So when I suggested dinner one evening, she accepted provided it was somewhere where she wouldn't be known. Poor Madge hadn't been so lucky with her marriage as I had. Sure, she had everything, in a material sense, but whatever affection she and Higgins once had died long ago. Even her son was a trial to her, although she tried to give him all the love that she had bottled up inside her. Perhaps there was too much of Higgins's blood in him. The boy just took, and gave nothing back. Until I met her again I think she had just about given up, and was going through the motions of life, trapped, with no hope, poor kid.'

Walsh dug his pipe out of his pocket and filled it, then, holding the flame of his lighter to it, puffed clouds of white smoke into the atmosphere.

Hammond paused to sip his drink and to light a cigarette.

A movement of air brought both clouds of smoke over to Brenda. She got up and moved to the chair opposite.

'Sorry,' they both said in unison.

'It's not your fault,' she murmured, 'it's me. The stuff is attracted to me like a wasp to jam.'

They both looked at her, suspiciously.

'You were saying?' she said sweetly, looking at Hammond.

'Oh yes. So I invited her to dinner. I took a room in the hotel in Newmarket, to save her having to get a pass into this place. I thought it was far enough away from Cambridge, so that nobody would know her. So there it was. She came and we had dinner, the night her husband was killed. The hotel staff will confirm it for you, if you ask them, I'm sure. So you see, she was with me that evening, you don't have to think that she had anything to do with it, but how's that for loyalty? She never said a thing to you, just to protect me from scandal. That's really something in a person, now isn't it?' he said, lost in admiration.

'It certainly is,' agreed Walsh. 'What time did she arrive at the hotel?'

'Must have been about half nine, quarter to ten, I should

101

think. You see, she had to go to a party beforehand. One of those charity sort of events, but she planned to arrive early and then sneak out when the bustle started, so no one would miss her. We were the last to be served in the dining-room, and definitely the last to finish,' he added.

'What time would that be, then? These country hotels don't keep their dining-rooms open too late in the evening,' Walsh asked innocently.

'You're too darned right there. They weren't exactly rude to get us out of the dining-room, but they missed only by a whisker. Same in the bar; that was closing too. So I had to take some bottles up to my room. Must have been half eleven, nearly quarter to twelve,' Hammond replied.

'You mean that was the time she left you?' Walsh asked, a little startled.

'No, no, that was the time we finished the meal,' he replied impatiently. 'That's what you asked, wasn't it? No, we got talking about the old days, and it was nearer three when she left, just before perhaps, something like that, anyway. We'd both had a bit too much to drink by then. She made some coffee to sober herself up before she left. Things had got, well, a bit emotional by then, I suppose you might say. It had been such a marvellous evening for both of us. Well, that's what happened that night.'

Hammond leaned back in his chair and lit another cigarette. 'I shall come back when this has all blown over. She must be so lonely, poor kid. There's no need for you to tell her what I've told you, is there? I'd much prefer you didn't, but that's up to you, of course. I feel happier knowing that you don't have her on your suspect list any more. I'd have spoken to you earlier, but I've been so busy, and it wasn't until yesterday that I had a chance to ring her again. That's when I found out about the Professor's death. Came as a hell of a shock, I can tell you, but I slept on it and I've done the right thing for both of us but I can't get over her trying to protect me.'

102

He was still wondering over this phenomenon when they left him.

'Trouble is,' Walsh said, as they drove back, 'what he told us doesn't take her off the list at all. It rather moves her up a place. An old flame turns up and gets all sentimental, giving her a last chance of a life of love and companionship. Only her husband stood in the way. That doesn't explain where Varney comes in, though, I admit, and she doesn't seem the type to want to romp with him, not of her own free will, but if we could find some real link between him and her, I'd think we were nearly home and dry. Pity the print on that button Packstone found was too smudged to get a comparison. Maybe we'll find that something else has cropped up when we get back.'

'He's all right, Mrs Holmes, I don't mind. They need to let off steam at their age, don't they?' Brenda said, easing the grubby little three-year-old to a sitting position beside her on the settee.

'They're getting a bit of a handful. I'll be glad when he starts school, but that's not till next year, I'm afraid. Here, let me wipe his nose, you don't want that on your clean jeans, oh, and he's got sticky hands. There, that's better.' Mrs Holmes looked tired and harassed.

'You were saying that your husband, Robin, doesn't go out much,' Brenda prompted.

'No, poor chap. I get so tired these days, what with the children and the housework, the washing, the ironing and the cooking, let alone the shopping as well. Mind you, Robin's ever so good, he helps as much as he can, baths the kids and gets them to bed so's I can have a bit of a rest, and he'll go up the supermarket in the evenings for me. I can't complain, but we've no time to get out and enjoy ourselves, even if we could afford it, which we can't. Robin's not that well paid, you see, and by the time we've paid the mortgage and the HP on the car and the video, there's nothing left. It's a jolly good thing Robin grows all the vegetables we need on his allotment, else things'd be even worse,' she said, running her hand over her pale, freckled forehead and through her yellowish, ginger hair.

'An allotment? That sounds a lot of hard work!'

'Yes, it is, but he enjoys it. He's down there most Sunday mornings, and the odd hour or two in the evenings, more if he's got the time or there's something needs doing bad.'

'You said he didn't go out on those two evenings I've asked you about, but did he go down the allotment, by any chance?'

Mrs Holmes rubbed round her eyes, a little helplessly. 'Might have, I don't remember for certain, what with one thing and another. No, Johnny! I don't think the lady does want that toffee, not after you've been sucking it.'

12

'Well, how did you get on with Mrs Dubonnet?' Walsh asked Sergeant White in a friendly voice.

'I've written out my reports, sir, covering the points you wanted checked out, but I thought I'd just have a word and mention something that I felt was strange. It might be important, or it might not be, but I thought I'd mention it, just in case,' White told him.

'Hang on a minute, then.' Walsh picked up the phone and rang the duty sergeant. 'Get Sergeant Walters on the phone for me, would you, please? As soon as you can.' He turned back to Sergeant White. 'I haven't had time to read anything yet, so you might as well fill me in. What have you turned up?'

'Well, I interviewed all the people who had attended Mrs Dubonnet's sessions on the night of Higgins's death, since you were obviously anxious to check out her alibi. Those that attended earlier in the evening confirmed their times with no problem. It was the last session's people that seemed strange to me. There were only three of them, and although they were all convinced that they had in fact gone to see her that evening, each of them had a calendar or diary on which they had written that their session was for the night before. None of them could account for it, although it didn't make them doubt what they'd told me. If there had only been one out of three, I probably wouldn't have thought anything of it. As it was, I felt it was highly suspicious, her being a hypnotist, you see. So I set out to try and confirm what they said, by talking to others in their families and the neighbours, but I haven't found any positive corroboration. So I got the names of those who attended her sessions the night before, and checked them out as well. There were only two anti-smokers, and they both said they were the only ones there at that time, but I'm convinced, myself, that there's a possibility that all five were at the earlier session and while they were under the influence, she made some of them believe they were attending on a different date. The neighbours are so used to the comings and goings that they can't recall the details for any particular evening. So whether Mrs Dubonnet went out that evening or not, I still don't know. I'm sorry, I've neither confirmed her alibi nor knocked it down, only cast more doubts,' White announced, slightly aggressively.

'What about the night Varney died?'

'Two sessions of three, finished about nine, confirmed by all six. So she could have done that one.'

'Don't worry about it. You're after facts, and sometimes things turn out this way. Did you find out any connection with Varney?' Walsh inquired.

'Oh yes. Certainly I did. There were a number of University employees, all trying to give up smoking. They came as a group, and Varney was one of them. I've written their names down in my report. That was after Higgins had had his machine made, whatever it is, so at least I've been helpful in that respect. I found out a bit about Mrs Dubonnet, though. She's been living there for some years, and her neighbours like her and her husband. They feel sorry for them. The husband was a national serviceman on Christmas Island, when they tested the hydrogen bombs, you see. Now he's dying of leukaemia. They've tried hard to get some compensation out of the government, but with no success, as you can imagine. Mrs Dubonnet even raised a petition locally and involved the local Member of Parliament. That's why everyone knows about her. It earned her a lot of local sympathy. That's why they didn't take too kindly to my nosing around. Still, that's what I'm paid for. I've got it all in my report, but I just wanted to make sure that you understood about those smokers the night Higgins died,' White added earnestly.

The phone rang.

'You wanted me, I believe, sir,' Sergeant Walters said.

'That's right,' Walsh replied. 'We've had a fellow phone up to say that Mrs Higgins spent the evening her husband was killed with him. Check out his story for me.' Walsh gave him the details of times and the hotel in Newmarket.

'Good. I'm glad you've come up with something, sir. I've been banging my head against a brick wall all day and getting absolutely nowhere fast. I'll drop a report in later,' Walters replied.

Reginald Finch's wife, Margaret, was helping Gwen in the kitchen; Walsh was with Reg and Brenda in the lounge.

'I'm afraid Marion Dubonnet is high on the list at the moment,' Walsh said reluctantly.

'You said the same of Mrs Higgins this morning, Chief,' murmured Brenda, as she sipped sherry from one of Walsh's best crystal glasses.

'I know I did, but there's a better connection between Varney and Mrs Dubonnet than between Varney and Mrs Higgins. He only met Mrs Higgins just the once, as far as we know, so the chance of a conspiracy there is highly tenuous. There isn't anyone else, except Higgins, who's a common factor in both cases and he couldn't have murdered Varney, could he? So there's only Mrs Dubonnet.'

'You're wrong, boss,' Finch announced. 'You haven't got around to reading young White's report yet. He gives a list of the people from the laboratory who went on the anti-smoking sessions with Varney. Well, there's a name there that's common to both cases and that's a fellow called Harrison.'

Both Brenda and Walsh looked at him curiously.

'Go on,' Walsh asked.

'There was a Harrison that attended the same reception that Mrs Higgins went to. You're not saying that that's the same man that works at the labs, are you, Reg?' Brenda asked.

'Got the same initials and lives at the same address as the fellow that you interviewed. Might just be the same man, and neither of you have mentioned the lab director – he knew them both, too,' Reg replied with a grin.

'Of course we knew about the director, Reg. Come on, what time did Harrison get to and leave the reception? Stop mucking us about,' Brenda grumbled.

'He got there at eight thirty and left just after eleven,' Reg replied.

'It only takes a few minutes to get from there to the Higgins' house. He could have left the reception and gone back, Chief,' Brenda added.

Walsh relit his pipe.

'You're quite right, he could have done it, and the director could have nipped out of his bridge party. I suppose it's because of Varney's sex partner, but I've been developing the preconception that we're after a woman. It could have been a male friend, but neither the director nor Harrison are beneficiaries of Higgins's estate, so there is no direct monetary motive. If either of those two had wanted Higgins's machine, why would they get involved with Varney?'

'Perhaps Varney knew one of them wanted it badly, so he got it himself, then offered it at a price. A price one of them wasn't prepared to pay,' suggested Brenda.

'That's possible. We must check out their alibis for the

night of Varney's murder. I can't remember what they were offhand,' Walsh said, rubbing his chin thoughtfully.

'I've only been through everything once, so far,' Reg admitted. 'The trouble is, the reports are coming in so fast I've not had a chance to start again from the beginning. So often there's things in the earlier reports that only become significant when you know what comes later. Sounds a bit Irish, but you know what I mean.'

'It's not helped by having this security element thrown in on top of everything else. Part of my mind is continuously worrying about what the devil that machine is going to be used for next. That doesn't help to create a balanced view of the evidence,' Walsh admitted.

'Bit of luck that American phoning in, though, boss, wasn't it?' Reg suggested. 'It would have taken a hell of a lot of leg work to have found that all out. What was Hutchinson's reaction at MI5, or whatever they call themselves, when you asked him to find out about Major Hammond?'

'He didn't like the suggestion of American involvement, but in his opinion they wouldn't have allowed Hammond to get in touch with us at all if they were really involved. So I wound him up by stressing the coincidence. Here's Higgins, developing something interesting, and lo and behold, out of the blue comes the old flame to chat up his wife. Hammond gets her well out of the way, then someone goes into Higgins's house to pick up the working data from the computer. I think Hutchinson's loath to stir up trouble; anyway, it's given him something to think about,' Walsh told him.

'You certainly make all your theories sound highly probable, Chief. Which one do you lay your money on, at this stage?' Brenda asked.

'All of them,' Walsh replied with a laugh. 'Just wait a bit, we might find some link between the Iraqis or the Libyans and Harrison. What odds would the bookies give then, do you think?'

'Wouldn't like to think, Chief,' Brenda said, with a relaxed, musical chuckle.

'Come on, you three, the food's on the table. Pour the wine, please, Sidney,' Gwen said, her face just slightly flushed from the heat of the kitchen.

The highly polished mahogany dining-room table was a picture of elegance. Crystal glasses sparkled in the candlelight, silver cutlery shone and colourful Wedgwood porcelain plates and dishes glowed richly. The aroma of good food wafted and teased the appetite.

'Wow!' exclaimed Brenda excitedly. 'Straight out of *Homes and Gardens.*'

'You sit there, Brenda, next to me. Margaret, you next to Sidney, and you, Reg, next to me on the other side. Right, here we go, I hope you all like mushrooms,' Gwen said.

'They smell great. What's the sauce, Gwen?' Reg inquired.

'Just garlic butter, Reg, and some spices. I'm sorry if it's going to mess up your romantic life, the smell, I mean.'

'I thought garlic was an aphrodisiac,' Walsh commented.

'Just like men, the conversation's already round to sex, and we've only just started,' Gwen replied.

'That's a bit more interesting than what's been on the telly all week, though,' Margaret added.

'You mean the party conference, at Blackpool? I did watch a bit. Very little new, though, most of it's a repeat of last year. All the conferences are the same, they're just an excuse for politicians and their wives to wine and dine. It's a shame that most of the speakers find it necessary to use bad grammar and flowery adjectives, just to talk down to their listeners. You'd have thought that the idea of the working man being thick was outdated by now. Don't you think so, Brenda?' Gwen asked.

'Yes, I agree with you. Perhaps they've formed themselves into such a tight clique that they copy each other's behaviour,' she replied.

'That's interesting,' Walsh remarked. 'Have you considered the possibility that they all went on the same public-speaking courses?'

He rose to collect the used plates. Gwen slipped out at the same time, to fetch plates of steak chasseur. Walsh brought in dishes of vegetables: peas, carrots and sweetcorn, all steaming.

'Brenda, please help yourself,' Gwen asked, hurrying out for the tureen of creamed potatoes while her husband walked round topping up the glasses.

'Frankly, boss, all the political parties can go to pot as far as I'm concerned, when there's a meal like this in front of me. Gwen, you're a gem. The boss is a real lucky guy to have got his hooks in you. If Margaret wasn't around, I wouldn't mind trying to dislodge him,' Reg remarked.

'That sounds like a compliment, and since I've found in life that they are very rare, I'm going to hang on to that one.'

'That's not fair, love,' Sidney protested. 'I'm always telling you what a wonderful person you are.'

'Yes, dear,' she smiled at him, 'but when you get to my age, it's nice to hear it from someone else as well, even if it's only to do with my cooking.'

'I hope I look as young as you do, when I'm your age,' Brenda added hesitantly.

'You're wearing very well, dear, all things considered.' Sidney Walsh smiled at his wife.

'It's very nice to see you and Margaret again, Reg. How are you finding your course?' Gwen inquired, to change the subject.

'It varies – it's either very boring or very interesting, but I wasn't unhappy to get called back. Which reminds me, boss, you asked for me for three days. Well, we were due for a mid-course break anyway, so I'm free until Thursday, if you want. If you don't, I'll have to do boring things like playing golf or watching the telly. Can't go away anywhere, because of Margaret working.'

'I'm sure we can keep you interested, don't you think so, Brenda?' Sidney responded jovially.

'Certainly looks like it, Chief. I haven't said how grateful I am to you for inviting me here tonight. A wonderful meal and good company. It's marvellous,' Brenda said, so sincerely that a couple of delicate little tears trickled down her blushing cheeks. A couple of glasses of wine often made her head swim, something a girl usually needed to be careful of, but tonight there was no need to worry. She settled down to enjoy herself.

13

There was a faint drizzle in the air and the wiper blades juddered noisily across the smeary windscreen as the car was driven slowly round the dark, twisting bends of the narrow road. The driver peered forward through the gloom. Just ahead was the entrance to the pub car-park. Gravel crunched under the wheels as he drove cautiously through the area bathed in the pale yellow light from the entrance doors and made for the darker spaces, along by a high hedge leading down to the river. As the car turned its headlights were reflected, momentarily, on the slowly moving black water.

There were several cars there, not surprisingly, considering that it was a Saturday night, but he thought he saw the one that he expected to meet. Good, he had begun to fear that it might all have been a mistake.

When he had posed his question, it had really been as a bit of a joke, he hadn't really expected to be taken seriously. The other person's eyes had looked away at first, then were raised to gaze directly into his with that disconcerting stare. Then those eyes had opened slightly wider, until he had found himself feeling as though he was falling into their deep, sparkling emptiness. They held such promise of sensation and wonder. He had been aware of the pink tip of a tongue showing between the soft, slightly parted lips.

'I'll tell you all about it, but somewhere private, very private,' the voice had whispered, low and husky.

He'd been keyed up with anticipation ever since, and it had been hard to hide his excitement during the day.

Alice, his wife, had no time for that sort of thing now, though once things had been different. She hadn't even bothered to ask where he was going when he had said that he was just popping out.

He switched off the lights and the engine. Let the other person come to him, that was good psychology. It would help to set up his dominance. He leaned back and wriggled to ease his trousers, which had pulled tight round his backside. As he did so, the thought that the other's hand might reach over to touch him there caused his face to flush and his cheeks to feel warm. Oh, the gentle touch of those fingers as they lightly moved over him, working their way to undo buttons and zips. He groaned and writhed as he imagined the cool, soft hand touching the warm flesh, the fingers moving, reaching for him. Like the hand of that young hitch-hiker he'd given a lift to last year. It had been very late, and such a cold and wet night that the hitch-hiker hadn't had a lot of choice. He had fumbled and grasped the other, while he had moaned and writhed as the hiker's hands caressed him. All too quickly his passion had risen and burst away, leaving that blessed feeling of satisfaction and contentment. The other had given a giggle of relief at having escaped so easily.

That seemed ages ago.

There was still no movement yet from the other car, but he could wait no longer.

Leaving the keys in the ignition, he opened his door and walked slowly over the shingle.

The door of the other car opened.

He could see, in the faint light, a dark figure getting out and facing him, holding a black camera-like box. Then, suddenly, nothing at all.

*

The river and the common, on the far side of the boat houses, were covered by a wreathing, thin, white misty haze, which blended into a heavy grey sky. Occasionally the black figure of a cyclist would suddenly appear out of the fog, riding along one of the common's intersecting footpaths.

Traditionally, on Sunday mornings, the river was for the use of the townsfolk's rowing clubs, some of which used boats borrowed from the colleges. Figures moved about on the shingle hards in front of the boat houses, without haste, some carrying oars to lean against walls. Then, as time went by, the mist seemed to thin a little, and more figures appeared, by bicycle or on foot. They congregated for a time by the water's edge, most of them carrying cases or bags, then drifted by ones and twos into the buildings. At two boat houses particularly, activity seemed to quicken. Small groups in white shorts and singlets moved into the wide-open doors to reappear, moments later, like some monstrous multi-legged insect, with a long, brown, up-side-down rowing eight. They wheeled round at the water's edge. The boats were raised high, turned over and lowered into the river. Now the signs of a race between the two clubs became more apparent. Oars were hastily laid across the boats. The bow-side men gingerly seated them-selves and reached outwards to fasten the screws of their outrigger gates. Finally, with all the crew aboard, the small coxes, with scarves wrapped thickly round their necks and little peaked caps pulled tightly on their heads, stepped delicately aboard, and fumbled for the toggles of the steer-ing ropes, then the boats were pushed out from the bank.

The downstream eight, with pale blue painted blades, manoeuvred itself straight, after some shrill cries from the cox, and commenced a slow paddle down the river. Wait-ing cyclists on the other bank mounted their machines, megaphones slung behind their backs, and set off in pursuit. The second boat, with maroon-coloured blades, having lost the right to lead the morning's flotilla downstream, followed sedately behind.

For the first half-mile or so, the river was narrow and wound itself round slow bends, so the crews maintained a steady even rate, contenting themselves with settling into a rhythm and warming their chilly muscles. There was no need for haste at this stage. Before the first long straight section of the river, the coaches on their bicycles needed to cross over on the last of the footbridges to get on to the towing path proper. The crews rested on their oars while this took place.

There were not many spectators about; it was still relatively early. A few dedicated anglers, well wrapped in waterproofs, wisely wound in their lines, taking the opportunity to check their bait, and prepared to recast when the boats were past.

The coaches were now ready. The cox called for the bow oar to pull a half-stroke to straighten the boat, then all was ready for a practice racing start.

'Come forward,' the thin, piping voice of the cox screamed. 'Twenty strokes. Are you ready? Row!'

The boat leapt forward, wobbled uncomfortably, then steadied. The cox was counting the numbers, keeping a close eye on the blade of the stroke's oar in front of him.

'Well done, lads, keep it up,' boomed the hollow voice through a megaphone.

On the next stroke, number three's blade became entangled in a bundle of cloth floating just beneath the surface.

It all happened very quickly. He was unable to withdraw the blade; the butt of the oar swung up and knocked him flat on to his back. The oarsman behind came forward for his next stroke and his bent knees cracked into the head of

116

the sprawling number three. Taken by surprise, he sent his own blade into the water at the wrong angle. The speed of the boat dug it deep, twisted the loom from his grip and swung it round viciously to smack into his jaw.

Water splashed in over the gunwales as the boat lurched wildly, rocking first to one side then the other.

'Easy all! Hold it!' screamed both cox and coach.

The boat veered round, in spite of the cox's frantic pulling on the steering ropes, then rammed the bank of the towing path, slewing across the flow of the river.

The following boat had taken the opportunity to compare its own racing start performance with that of the boat in front, and had done rather too well.

In spite of its own screamed emergency stop procedure, there was just no river space for it. Its cox, in desperation, pulled his tiller ropes hard over, and ran his bow into the opposite bank. Then his boat swung round and joined the chaos.

The offending bundle of cloth drifted gently downstream. In response to an angry shout from the cyclists, an oar was used to push it towards the bank, but it was larger than it at first appeared and a second oar gave an additional thrust, causing the bundle to turn over. A white hand appeared momentarily above the surface. The faces of the nearest oarsmen turned just as pale, and there was a gulping sound as one of them brought up the partially digested contents of his stomach into the turgid waters of the sluggishly flowing river.

The body was pushed to the bank, where the combined efforts of the reluctant coaches, their bicycles left lying in a heap on the towing path, were needed to drag the dripping corpse up on to the grass. It took several minutes for them to collect their wits and to get themselves sorted out.

Eventually one of the cyclists rode off, back up the towing path, to a telephone box and the nervous thrill of dialling 999.

By the time he returned, having waited for the police and ambulance to arrive, the two boats had got themselves alongside the river bank.

The unfortunate oarsman still groaned with the pain of his dislocated jaw and was swathed with all the scarves and coats that could be found. His colleague sat by him on the bank, dejectedly holding his head in his hands.

The police patrol man became flustered after the body had been laid on a stretcher. 'You two crews had best get back to your boat houses. I'll need to take statements from you, and we can't do it here.'

He watched as his mate and the coaches helped the injured to walk to the ambulance, while he remained to help push the boats away from the bank. The one with the light blue blades, its two spare oars hanging limply from their outriggers, crept listlessly against the stream, back upriver.

The police patrol men had forgotten to search the pockets of the clothing on the body for some means of identification. They had intended to, but by the time they had returned to their car, the ambulance had already left. So they went to take statements from the disconsolate crewmen before going to report at HQ. By this time the ambulance had been out to the hospital with the injured oarsmen, and had taken the body to the mortuary.

It was therefore nearly two hours before news reached Detective Chief Inspector Walsh that the body which had been fished out of the River Cam, apparently drowned, was that of Alan Harrison, the short, tubby, middle-aged man with the thinning fair hair: the personnel officer at the laboratory where once George Varney had been employed.

'What the hell is going on, Sidney? It's playing havoc with our statistics. Three in a week! It's more like a bloody massacre. What the devil are you doing about it?' The C.C.'s irate voice thundered over the telephone.

'I don't know how Harrison died yet, sir, or whether it relates to Higgins and Varney, though the probability is high. It rather looks as though the killer's getting rattled. Maybe he'll have made a big mistake this time,' Walsh said hopefully.

'I don't know if the killer's getting rattled. I know I bloody well am. Report to me later, when you know a bit more.'

Walsh sat thoughtfully for a moment. 'Reg, get Sergeant White checking on Harrison's alibi for the night Varney died, and those times Harrison said he arrived and left Councillor Stevens' party. Find out if anyone saw him leave early and come back again. Yes, and get his car's number and its description, we'll assume he drove himself to his death, so his car must be near the river somewhere. He'd never get over the Jesus Green weir, so get a team looking downstream from there. Come on, Brenda, we're for the morgue. We might just as well make sure he's been murdered before we drive ourselves nutty.'

But the rubber-cloaked pathologist and the police doctor had not decided on precisely what they had found.

'Certainly he was drowned, no question of that,' the pathologist said.

'And certainly in the river,' added the doctor, 'but I think he drowned while unconscious.'

'So do I,' the pathologist agreed, 'but why was he unconscious? You'd expect some marks indicating he had struck his head or something, and he was stone sober too, not touched a drop. His clothes were barely dishevelled too, except for a loosened tie.'

'Would you say that he might have been in a trance, a hypnotic state, for instance?' Walsh asked resignedly.

119

Both the doctor and the pathologist looked at him thoughtfully for a few moments.

'Yes,' the pathologist answered eventually, 'it's possible, up to a point, but a trance state must be caused by something specific, alcohol, drugs or something similar, and there are no such traces in this body. A hypnotic state would be unlikely to have survived the shock of a sudden immersion in cold water, not in my experience, but having said that, I don't feel it can be ruled out completely. What do you think doctor?'

'I'd go along with that, with the reservation that a hypnotist doesn't just create trances, there's also the possibility of the suggestion being planted in his mind. A man might be convinced he could jump off a ten-storey building safely. He dies, of course, but what if the thought was planted in his mind that he could hold his breath under water for ten minutes, for instance, or even that he could breathe under water? What then? We might end up with the symptoms as in this case,' the doctor suggested.

'Could his head have been held under, while he was in a trance, then?' Walsh asked eager to try and clarify this vagueness.

Both men turned back to the body for a few moments.

'If it was, then it was not held down with any force. There's no marks, you see,' the pathologist stated blandly.

'But if he was lying on the river bank and his head was held under, that would account for his tie being loosened, wouldn't it?' Brenda asked

'It could, all other things being equal. In which case there may be traces on his clothes that might confirm that. I'm very curious. We'll do some more work on it. Give us a bit more time, Inspector.' He turned away with his hand on the doctor's shoulder. 'What about the pupils of the eyes? Let's have another look. Interesting case this, you know.

Maybe we should write this one up for the medical journal. What do you think?'

*

'Would the state of mind induced by Higgins's machine on a healthy person enable someone to drown him?' Walsh asked Hutchinson over the phone. 'Or would sudden immersion in cold water break the trance and cause the person to struggle for survival?'

'You want to know whether he would remain passive under those circumstances? Well, that's not a question I'd like to answer off the top of my head, Inspector. I'll need a little time to consider that. Give me a couple of hours. You've got another body, then?' Hutchinson inquired laconically.

'I have.'

'Things are really hotting up, aren't they?'

*

14

There was a neglected look about the pebble-dashed semi-detached house in the tree-lined avenue where Harrison had lived. Leaves littered the pavements and glistened in the damp atmosphere. The wooden slats were loose in the cross members of the flimsy wooden gate, from which most of the paint had peeled away, and the bottom scraped over the flinty concrete path as Walsh pushed it open. A few faded roses looked lost in the low jungle of weeds in the front garden.

The door was opened by a short, thin woman wearing large gold-framed spectacles and dressed in black; her hair was pulled tightly back from her forehead and knotted in a bun. Her eyes were slightly reddened and there was a worried look on her face.

'You'd better come in,' she said, after Walsh had introduced himself.

'We're sorry to disturb you, after such distressing news,' Walsh said sympathetically, watching her face.

'The Lord works in mysterious ways,' she said tonelessly. 'He has seen fit to take Alan away from me, into a far better place, leaving me here to carry on His work for Him. The Lord giveth and the Lord taketh away, blessed be the name of the Lord.'

'Very true, Mrs Harrison, very true. What time was it when your husband went out last night?' Walsh asked.

'It was gone half-past nine, of that I'm sure. The news was over; I thought that was why he went out. He had this thing about television, you see. He thought it made people into mindless morons, but he was quite happy to watch it himself if there was something he wanted to see. It was all right then. He never usually stayed out long, though. I'd hear him come in later and go up to his bedroom. He slept in the front, you see, and I have the back. I'd not see him again until morning. What time did I go to bed last night? About eleven. I could see the light in his room from under the bottom of the door. I never went in, of course, our relationship had got on to a higher plane than that sort of thing, but I never gave it a thought to look outside to see if the car was there. It was the same this morning. I was up and ready to go to our meeting by half ten, and he hadn't shown himself by then, but that wasn't unusual. He often had a lie-in on the Lord's Day. So I didn't think to. You wouldn't, would you? I mean, there was no reason why I should, was there? Even when I got back and saw that the car wasn't there, I didn't think anything was wrong. It wasn't until one of your chaps came round that I realized. I feel so guilty about it. It's proper upset me, it has. Just to think that he fell into the river and drowned, and I hadn't even missed him. Not that there would have been much I could do about it, of course. He was already dead by then, if you understand me, but it's the not knowing. Like no one cared for him, that's what upsets me so much. He wasn't drunk, was he?'

Walsh shook his head.

'No, of course, he wouldn't be. There'll be an inquest, won't there? I'd be ever so grateful if you'd ask the coroner man to make a special point of saying that. It's the neighbours, you see, and all my friends. They'll all think he was drunk, and I wouldn't like that at all.'

'Are you saying that you had no idea where he was going when he went out last night? You don't know where he

went or if he was going to meet anybody?' Walsh interrupted, trying to curb his impatience.

She shook her head.

'Had he been acting strangely in any way? Had he said
whether anything was upsetting him, or worrying him,
then?' Walsh asked.

'Well, no. You see we didn't talk much about things and I
didn't notice.' She started to sob quietly. 'I should have
been there to hold his hand while he died. That's how it
should be done. If I'd known, I would have, of course I
would,' she mumbled to herself.

'May I go upstairs and look in his bedroom? There may be
something that might tell us something.'

'Go and look if you want to. The front bedroom,' she
replied.

'You stay here, Brenda, and talk to Mrs Harrison. I'll go
on my own,' Walsh whispered.

There was a single bed with a patchwork quilt, which
hadn't been slept in. An old-fasioned bedroom suite of
veneered walnut, rather chipped in places, took up much
of the remaining space.

A library book lay open on a white bedside cabinet, with
a copy football coupon as a bookmark. In a small drawer he
found a writing pad and envelopes, some ballpoint pens,
and a nearly empty packet of cigarettes with an ashtray.
The lower cupboard contained a dozen or more glossy
magazines. Walsh's nose wrinkled in disgust: weird, erotic
poses, mostly men, some of them only young boys. Walsh
shook his head. He'd already visualized, having met the
wife, that Harrison probably suffered frustrations of some
sort, but he hadn't imagined this sort of thing.

He turned his attention to the dressing-table and the
wardrobe, but found nothing of interest other than a diary
with an entry for the previous day, written in blue ballpoint, just saying '10 p.m?'

He went downstairs.

'Did your husband have any friends that he might have gone to visit, Mrs Harrison?' he asked.

Her hands were held together as if in prayer. Her head shook slightly. 'I don't think he'd got any. Now if he'd come to our meetings he might have made some. Most of his friends have moved away over the years. Sometimes he would have to go to meetings in the evenings to do with the laboratory, but that wasn't often, really. He never said anything to me, I've no idea what he could have been up to,' she replied.

'Well, thank you for being so helpful, Mrs Harrison. If you do happen to think of anything that you think would be useful, ring me at this number, please.' He handed her his card. 'Now, is there anything we can do to help you? We will, if we can,' he said kindly.

'No! It's all right, thank you. I shall be having some friends arrive soon, who'll understand. I'll be all right.'

As the front door closed behind them Brenda told Walsh that Harrison's car had been found. 'HQ rang through while you were upstairs. It's in the car-park of a pub down near the towing path, in Chesterton,' she said.

The sky was brightening a little, and some breaks were appearing in the low grey clouds.

A panda car was parked near Harrison's grey Metro in the pub car-park. A young, uniformed policewoman got out and came over.

'This is Harrison's car, sir,' she told them. 'The keys are still in it, but there's nothing else that I can see. The finger-print men have just left, sir. They told me to tell you they'd drop a report into your office. I've taken a statement from the landlord, but he isn't very helpful. I've tried to find out what cars were here last evening, but he says he hasn't been here long. Most of the locals he has got to know walk here.'

'Very good, I'll see the landlord myself in a minute. Have you spoken to the people in those houses opposite yet?' he asked.

The girl shook her head.

'Not yet, sir. I didn't think you would be long in coming, so I've been sitting in the car writing up the notes of what I've learned so far.'

'Make a start now. I'll get someone here to help you, if you like, and I want you to come back here this evening, in plain clothes, and question all those that turn up in the bars. Someone might have seen Harrison, or something unusual. The duty sergeant will tell you what to do if you've any doubts,' Walsh instructed.

'I can manage on my own, really I can, sir,' she replied earnestly.

'All right then, hand in your written reports before you go off duty.'

Walsh turned his attention to the car.

There was nothing there to interest him, so he went to find the landlord.

'Well, I don't know what else to say. I've already told the policewoman all I know about it, and frankly, that's nothing at all. I saw the car there this morning, but I didn't give it that much thought, even after all that kerfuffle this morning down on the towing path, when they found his body. There's often a car or two gets left behind of a night, when someone thinks they might have had a bit too much and gets afraid of the old breathalyser. They call a taxi, and pick up their car next morning. So I didn't think anything of it until your woman comes in this lunchtime, asking questions about it,' the landlord said hurriedly, wanting to get back to his usual Sunday afternoon nap. He'd be tired for the evening session if he didn't. Didn't people realize how important a kip in the afternoon was to a busy publican?

'I'll be having two of my people down here this evening

126

to talk to your customers. You needn't worry, they'll be discreet and in plain clothes, but I've got to find out if any of them saw anything.'

The landlord looked at him reluctantly. He'd have liked to have told this Inspector to go jump in the river, but that wouldn't do him any good, there was always the licensing authority to worry about, and the police could make things difficult for him.

'Only too pleased to help,' he replied.

Brenda had wandered down to the water's edge and stood watching the litter on the sluggish, dark green river as it flowed slowly by. Walsh walked over to her, his feet crunching the shingle and his hands in his pockets. The tall privet hedge, which grew along one side of the car-park, reached far out over the river at the end, and trailed several long branches in the water. Up against these, the stream had built up an oily area of flotsam, dead leaves and other rubbish. The water level was quite high, only an inch or two below the top of the long row of paving slabs that edged the bank. He crouched down to study the slabs nearest to the hedge. The dirt there was disturbed. Were those the marks of a man having his head held under the water? A couple of scratches further back could have been caused by the toe caps of the man's shoes.

He turned round and looked towards the path. With a few cars backed up to the hedge, this corner would be well out of the view of anyone moving about over there; add to that the effect of someone looking out of a lighted area towards the darkness of the hedge. A safe spot, then, for a murder.

He spoke to HQ on the panda car's radio. Packstone's forensic men would be out again to take samples of the dirt. They would find out if there were any traces on Harrison's clothes to match them.

Walsh felt tired and a little confused, but there were more

reports to come in yet. Maybe then the answers would start to slot into place. On the other hand, maybe they wouldn't.

'I spent a long time going round the route young Varney must have took, sir. It weren't difficult, though. When I came to ask questions there were quite a few people about in the village at the time, and they noticed things. Nothing like a village for knowing what goes on, is there? There's three in Coton, and two in the other villages, that saw him on his moped and they all say he was on his own, definitely no one with him. So you won't get to your killer that way, sir, I'm afraid,' Sergeant Witherspoon said, laying down his file and notebook on the corner of Walsh's desk.

Walsh shrugged his shoulders.

'I can't say I'd pinned a lot of hopes on it, Sergeant, but at least I can cross that off the list of possibilities.'

'Now, the person on the blue moped. That bike was made in Indonesia, would you believe, sir?' Witherspoon confided.

'Really?'

'That's right. Mind you, I had to call on a couple of dozen places before I found out myself. There ain't many dealers, that make hasn't caught on at all well. Shop in Chesterton is the only one in the whole of Cambridgeshire, the nearest other one's in Luton, and I haven't bothered with that one yet. They've only sold a dozen in the three years since they've had the franchise, not very good, is it? Still, only two of them were blue, so it's got to be one of those, I reckon. I've got the names here, one's a chap out Ely way, the other's a woman in Sawston. I haven't seen either of them yet, I haven't had the time, and tomorrow's my wife's aunt's funeral in Croydon. I can do it when I get back, if you like.'

'That's all right, Sergeant, you go off to your funeral.

128

We'll fit those calls in somehow. You've done well, thank you.'

'I hope you haven't done any deals with this motor-bike mob, Brenda,' Walsh said, giving her a very serious, inquisitorial look.

'Of course not, Chief, I wouldn't do a thing like that. I put the situation to them, and after a period of due consideration they agreed,' she replied innocently.

'Your silver tongue, I suppose. So where is this ambush being set up?'

Brenda pointed a slim finger to a spot on the map which lay open on Walsh's desk.

'That's the wood, and the bikes come in down this track here.'

'Pretty isolated, then. Your man could come in from either the north or the south, if he comes at all. You'd need a lot of men to cover an area that size, and even then you mightn't be certain of trapping him. We'd better see if we can narrow it down. Let's go and take a look at the ground. Nothing better than seeing for yourself, first hand.'

Walsh stood in the grassy glade in the centre of the copse. The early morning dew sparkled on his shoes and darkened his trousers near his ankles.

'Pretty isolated spot. Whereabouts was it that the girl got injured?'

'It was on the far side from where the track comes in. This way, I think, Chief,' Brenda replied.

The ground was uneven, and thickly overgrown with bushes and brambles through which soared mighty oaks, sycamores and other trees.

'Ah, I'm getting the picture. This is the site of an old

129

farmhouse, Brenda. Those ridges are all that's left of the walls, probably. That accounts for the big trees and just the one track in. Look, over there, an apple tree gone wild. This bit might have been a small orchard or vegetable patch. There's no building shown on the Ordnance Survey map, so it must have been deserted and well ruined in the early eighteen hundreds. Pity Reg isn't here, this is the kind of thing he likes to do.'

They followed a winding, narrow rabbit run towards the south, then walked round the copse to the north, looking for an existing way back in. There were two. Walsh's eyes looked keenly from side to side of the path as they walked in Indian file. Suddenly he stopped and pointed to his right at a few depressions in the tufty grasses.

'Someone's been that way recently. Let's see where he went. Tread carefully. We don't want to let everyone know we've been around.'

Walsh stepped unerringly, following the faintest of trails through the undergrowth. It was almost non-existent to Brenda's eyes, but after five or six yards they stood at the base of one of the oak trees still holding on to most of its curling and browning leaves, which rustled in the breeze.

'Your man wants a bird's-eye view this time, I think,' Walsh said casually, pointing at a number of six-inch nails that had been driven into the trunk at intervals of about eighteen inches, upwards towards the first of the stout branches.

'You're younger than I am, I'm past the age when climbing trees is fun. Pop up and see what's going on.'

With the nails as handholds and footholds, Brenda had no difficulty climbing, and once up amongst the branches almost disappeared from the view of someone on the ground.

'Super spot up here, Chief. I can see the glade down there perfectly,' she called to Walsh.

'Stay up there. I'll see if you can be seen from the open.'

He walked carefully round to the area where the young girl had undressed in the naked glare of the headlamps. 'I can't see you at all – oh well, not if you keep still, anyway. Come on down now,' he shouted.

'He's picked a nice comfy spot, Chief,' Brenda said, bending to try and brush dirty marks from her jeans. 'You reckon he'll get up there an hour or two beforehand, and stay till long after they've gone?' she asked.

'That's what I'd do, if I were him.'

15

As Brenda turned the car into the tree-lined avenue, the blue moped came out of the drive of one of the houses and headed down the road, leaving a trail of faint blue smoke.

'Blast,' she said, 'we've missed her.'

'Follow along behind, maybe she's only going to the shops,' Walsh growled.

But the bike went past the little row of village shops, turned down the road by the recreation ground near the church, and then disappeared through a gap in a hedge.

Brenda stopped. 'Can't follow her down there. I wonder where she's going?'

Walsh shrugged his shoulders.

'We'll have to walk to find out. It won't do us any harm. We're getting plenty of fresh country air this morning.'

They walked down the narrow path, avoiding the damp, muddy patches as best they could. Open fields stretched away to their left, and on their right was a thick high hedge. The wheel tracks were clear and easy to follow: they led to a gap in the hedge, a little wooden gate and the moped, half hidden in the bushes.

Walsh pushed open the gate into the untidy, overgrown, and virtually neglected allotments. Ivy climbed the ramshackle sheds, and wigwams of canes supported tendrils of dead peas and beans.

Walsh studied the muddy path for a moment then

headed towards a larger shed, away in a corner, backing on to the long hedge. Its glass windows were cracked and filthy, but the brass padlock was open and hanging loosely in the hasp.

Walsh reached for the door, pulled it open, and stared grimly at the startled couple sitting in the dim light on the narrow sack-covered bench along the far wall.

Robin Holmes's hand jerked out from beneath the woman's sweater. 'Here, what's the meaning of this? These allotments are private. Good Lord, you're that policeman. What do you want?' he said, in aggressive confusion.

'I think we want to have a few words with you two,' Walsh replied. 'You don't mind if we come in, do you? But I'll leave the door open, so we can see what we're doing.'

Walsh stepped inside, moved a rusty spade and sat down on an upturned bucket. Brenda found a dusty folding stool behind the door.

'Now we're all comfortable, I'll introduce us. Mrs Mannering, I'm Detective Chief Inspector Walsh, and this is Detective Constable Phipps. We're pursuing inquiries into the deaths of Professor Higgins, George Varney and Alan Harrison.'

'What! Alan Harrison? I didn't know that. Oh my gawd, the poor old sod. Why should anyone want to bump him off?' Holmes interrupted, in some alarm.

'That's right. Now, Mrs Mannering, we found this photograph in George Varney's flat. It is you, I presume?' He handed her the snapshot.

'Here, Rob, this is the one you took of me up near the golf course, isn't it?' she said, nudging her companion.

Holmes took it from her.

'S'right, I did. Here, that's mine. Good Lord, poor old George must have nicked it from my drawer in the lab. Maybe he fancied you, love.'

'Did you know George Varney, Mrs Mannering?' Brenda asked.

The woman shook her head. 'Only what Rob's told me about him. I've never actually met him.'

'So you think Varney took it from you? Now why would he do a thing like that?' Walsh asked Holmes.

'How the hell would I know? He had a moped of his own, maybe he saw Jill's picture in me drawer and fancied getting a girlfriend of his own, to go riding with. I can't ask him now, can I?'

'Hardly, but did he know of your, er, friendship with Mrs Mannering here?'

'I've never told no one. Look here, Inspector, you've got to understand, Jill and me's been friends for a long while now. We're both married and she's got kids too. Even if Jill's feller has bashed her up a few times, we can't just go off together, like we want to do. We've got responsibilities, but it ain't just that. How the hell could I afford to keep her kids as well as mine, and give money to my missus, she ain't got nothing and she's not well. We've talked it over, many times. We've got no choice but to keep going on as we are. One day the kids'll all be grown up, then maybe we can. No one knows we meet like this. You ain't going to let on about us, are you?' Holmes pleaded.

'He's right, sir,' Mrs Mannering added. 'Things aren't easy, but we're doing what we think best, and you'll cause an awful lot of problems if you do.'

'Your personal relationships are no concern of ours, Mrs Mannering: we're only concerned with tracking down a killer, but I'm afraid we're going to need to know a good deal more about you and your recent movements. So if you'll just be good enough to answer a few questions.'

The curtains at the front of the house were all drawn, even though it was midday.

Walsh rang the door bell, but it was several moments before Marion Dubonnet opened the door.

134

Her hair was untidy, her eyes were reddened and there was a listless droop to her shoulders. She stared in bewilderment for a little while, before she recognized her visitor.

'Come in,' she said.

Walsh followed her into the sitting-room.

'He's dead,' she stated bluntly, and it was Walsh's turn to look bewildered for a moment. 'He died the night before last, holding my hand. Even though I've been expecting it, it's still come as a shock.'

'I'm so sorry, Mrs Dubonnet,' Walsh replied, finding it was necessary to prevent his hand reaching out to her in sympathy.

'Tom was a good man, and a wonderful husband. The way I feel at the moment, I wish I could go with him.'

'That's very understandable, of course, but life goes on. It's easy to say that time's a great healer, but it is true. Are you here alone? You have got someone with you, haven't you?'

Mrs Dubonnet nodded. 'Everyone's been so kind. Joyce from across the road's been staying with me. She's just gone down to the shops. Did you want to see me about something?'

'Nothing important. I rather wanted a chat about some of your clients, but it can wait. I'll come back another day,' he said, thinking rapidly.

It was hardly appropriate, now, to ask her to account for her movements on the night before last, the night when Harrison was drowned, and her husband had died.

'He went in a good hour ago, sir, on the north side, just as you said,' the watcher, with the light-intensifier binoculars hanging round his neck, told Walsh.

'Right, you and Smith get round that side and follow in the way he went. We'll give you twenty minutes, then

Brenda and me'll start in from this side. Got your radios on earphones and throat microphones? Good, take it steady and quiet. You know where the tree is. If you get there first, wait a few yards out till we get there, then we'll flush him out together, OK?'

The other two crept off.

'The bikes'll be here in forty minutes, Chief. That should keep his attention, just as we close in,' Brenda whispered.

'If they keep to the timetable, and that's asking too much, in my opinion.'

Brenda shrugged her shoulders in the darkness. She'd set things up as best she could, but success would depend on many factors that were outside her control.

They waited in silence, then Walsh moved off, stealthily and silently. She did her best to do the same. Walsh seemed to have no problem finding the way. Bushes and trees loomed up in the gloom, and still they moved silently on, brambles snagging at her clothes, then Walsh's hand reached back to halt her.

They stood still.

A faint throbbing could be heard above the rustling of the leaves in the upper branches. Beams of light momentarily bathed the tree-tops ahead in silver and white. Walsh's hand guided, pushed her, to her left, towards the glade side of the tree. Then Smith's torch came on, illuminating the branches above and the shadowy figure crouched thirty feet up in the fork in the trunk.

'Come down! We're police! You're surrounded,' Smith shouted.

The figure scrambled down a few feet, then made a desperate bid for escape. He ran agilely along a huge branch, then leapt the twenty or so feet to the ground in the now illuminated glade, fell, got to his feet and ran, but all to no avail. He ran straight into the watcher and a flying dive from Brenda, but was lucky, all the same. He just avoided a swingeing, booted kick in the guts from the burly boy, who would have tried a few more in selected places had he been given the chance.

'I don't see why it needed four of you bleeding rozzers. She could've handled six of him, on her own,' he grumbled, pointing at Brenda.

'This is a normal video camera, sir. Nice one, though, with this zoom lens. It's not the black box you're after,' Smith said.

'Let's have a look at him,' interrupted Walsh.

John Higgins's chance of creating an exclusive, best-selling, pornograhic video had disappeared, for the time being.

'So you searched his house, did you? Find anything?' the Chief Constable asked.

'Yes,' Inspector Walsh replied. 'He's into pornography in quite a big way, all types too, but he's going to be mighty unpopular with some people for leaving his contact lists around. I'm not going to get involved, though. The Porn Squad can deal with it.'

'What the devil did he do with all the money his mum and dad gave him?'

'Ah, that's quite interesting. I told you John Higgins's wife was a bit left-wing. Well, there's more to it than that. It seems she's not the brightest piece around and she got herself into the position of funding all sorts of activities. Not just marches and demonstrations, but leaflets and the publication of a newspaper as well. No wonder old Higgins got mad when he found out where his money was going.'

'If John Higgins was hanging about in that wood last week, waiting for the Hell's Angels, he could hardly have been bumping his old man off. I suppose this puts him in the clear,' the C.C. suggested.

'I don't think so. After all, there's his wife to consider as well.'

The C.C. nodded wisely. 'Very true. Now, what are you doing about this Holmes and Mrs Mannering? Think there might be something in it?'

'I want to check up on the woman. It's possible they're trying to get the money together to make a break, and it certainly would account for Varney's involvement and the robberies in the villages but I'm not too sure. Holmes doesn't give me the impression of having enough bottle to tackle anything like that, particularly murder. The woman, well, that's a different kettle of fish. They're always tougher. She could have lied about knowing Varney, and there's the romp on the bed as well. I've not put that possibility aside.'

'You've got too many possibilities, Sidney. You're going to have to start eliminating some of them soon, if you want to get anywhere.'

Walsh shrugged. 'Maybe, but they'll have to eliminate themselves. Mrs Higgins is still well up the list. That American, Hammond, has gone back to the States, but he's mighty keen on her, no doubt about that, and her on him. They were together the night Varney died. No, that's no alibi for her, she'd still have plenty of time for that. She says she was at home when Harrison was drowned.'

'And the Dubonnet woman, her motive's nearly as good as Mrs Higgins's.'

Walsh nodded. 'We can't ignore any of them. Even the lab director's got money problems – gambling, I think.'

'What about the son of that cleaner, the woman that does the Higgins place, are you still interested in him?'

Walsh nodded. 'Him too.'

16

Reg Finch had papers and files all over the desk. He sat with his bottom lip trapped between his teeth, in deep concentration, marking off indexed summary sheets, cross-referencing them with original reports, as meticulously as any old-fashioned bookkeeper's auditor, with his coloured pencils. Each significant point of one report resulted in yet another report, either confirming it or otherwise. Every now and then it was necessary to summarize those aspects of the case still requiring verification, otherwise there was a risk that something might be overlooked, and not followed up. And if Murphy's law was anything to go by, that something would be the vital breakthrough.

'How's it going, Reg?' Brenda asked, closing the door slowly so as not to cause a draught.

Finch straightened his back and ran his hand through his fair hair. 'So so, I've seen worse. We've still got one or two items outstanding from the first briefing. Jones had the job of seeing Higgins's students and others in the colleges. One of the professors on friend Hughes's list had gone abroad, and hasn't been interviewed yet. It probably doesn't matter, since he wasn't around when the other two were killed, but it means I can't clear Jones's reports yet.'

'What's the professor's name? I've got to go and see Higgins's cleaner's son, Jim Byatt, again. The Chief's not happy about him yet. Maybe I can do the professor as well.'

'Good idea. I've got the chap's phone number some-where. I'll give him a ring and see if he's back yet, but you can't go and see a posh professor dressed like that, though, Brenda. Tatty jeans and T-shirt, you look more like a Hell's Angel's moll,' he said, grinning broadly.

Brenda scowled, and her eyebrows came together in a frown. 'Watch it, Buster.'

'Oh, hell, what now? I've told you everything I can,' Jim Byatt said, his face pale and worried.

'Perhaps, but I would like to go over what you've told us again,' Brenda replied impassively.

'My mum's not going to like you keeping on coming round here,' he warned.

'We'll see. Now, you say you went round with your mother to see the Professor. That was the week before he was killed, wasn't it?'

'Oh gawd, we've been through that before. All I did was give him one of our catalogues and introduce myself. He's got to get his computer stuff from somewhere, and I get commission on sales. I'd be daft not to try and get him to buy his stuff from us.'

'You went into his study, I understand.'

'That's right, that's where he'd got his installation. He was a decent old boy, nice enough to me, anyway. He said I could leave my price list and order form, and he'd see what he could do when he needed something next time, that's all. I don't see why you keep on about it. He was still alive when I left, you know that. Why can't you leave me alone?'

'While you were in his study, did you see any plans or drawings lying around? Did you see a black box, for in-stance, about the size of an old-fashioned camera?'

'Gawd, he'd got papers lying all over the place. I don't know what they were. You can't pick people's stuff up and read it, not in front of them. I think I saw a box thing, but I can't be certain. I didn't take that much notice.'

'On the night he was killed you say you were at football practice,' Brenda said, tapping her pen on the back of her hand.

'That's right, I was, and lots of people saw me there. You know, you've been round asking them.'

'Yes, but you went off jogging round the roads on your own, didn't you? Who can confirm what you did during that time? About an hour, wasn't it?'

Jim Byatt's face showed signs of panic. 'For Christ's sake, I've told you the truth. There must be dozens of people saw me running on me own. I don't know, how the hell can I? But there must be someone.'

'We haven't found anyone yet, I'm afraid. Now, two nights later, you say you drove to Huntingdon, to look at a used car in the forecourt of a garage. A Triumph TR7, I understand, but the garage was closed.'

'That's right, I did. I'm keen on sports cars, but you've got to be careful, there's a lot of dodgy dealers about. I wanted to see what condition it was in, but there was too much rust coming through the paint for my liking.'

'Again, there's no one who can confirm your story, is there?'

The boy looked crestfallen, and shook his head despondently.

'So that's what we'll do with those on the Probable list. Tomorrow morning, Reg, get together with the duty sergeant and try and make up some sort of surveillance roster. I know you'll have problems finding enough people, but do the best you can. We'll also get the assessments of their financial states checked, those that we haven't already done, that is,' Walsh announced, moving the papers on his desk to one side.

Brenda yawned and rubbed at her eyes. Finch rubbed a leg that had grown stiff from inactivity.

'Shall we have a break now?' Walsh suggested. 'I know it's getting late, but we've still got more to do. I don't fancy the canteen again, how about that little place down the road?'

A light drizzle was falling as they walked round the corner to the little restaurant. In spite of the damp weather, the small row of shops seemed to have attracted a surprising number of people, window-shopping on a Sunday evening.

They found a table away from the door. Neither of the two younger ones seemed keen to open a conversation, and Walsh was ready to lose himself in his own thoughts.

It was too easy to think that the murders might have been committed by someone that he hadn't even come across yet, and all his planning would be of no account. The development of the Science Park, in recent years, was specifically aimed at providing for the commercial development of clever ideas. That meant there were plenty of people in the city with the ability and imagination to appreciate the value of something like Higgins's hypnotizer. No, that wasn't quite right. Higgins's machine would never quite fit into that category. Obviously there would be a large market, if the politicians allowed such things to be manufactured and sold freely, but it would need a great stretch of the imagination to believe that their general use would ever be permitted. So – just where would a thief sell the gadget, then? It would need special contacts or a special organization. You would hardly expect a thief to draw up outside one of the London embassies in a taxi, walk in, and say, 'Hey, do you want to buy this thing? I've only killed three people to get it.' Possible, but not very likely. Surely, if a foreign power were involved, then it would have been involved right from the beginning and organized it all. Having said that though, they surely wouldn't hang about

142

Cambridge after they'd got it, would they? He could fit into that scheme the murders of both Higgins and Varney, but not that of Harrison. If Varney had caused problems by not handing it over when he should have, and got himself eliminated as a result, then they wouldn't hang about, but Harrison's death showed that that hadn't happened. Therefore the invention was still somewhere local.

'Come on, boss. What are you going to order?' Finch interrupted, jerking at his elbow.

The waiter was standing by the table, a seven o'clock shadow on his plump cheeks and a faint discoloration on the lapel of his black jacket, testament to some past culinary mishap.

Walsh blinked away any signs of irritation: his mind had been starting to work and do its job. He might have been on the verge of a solution. Would he be able to return to the same line of thinking? Already those thoughts were fading fast as he looked at the two grinning faces in front of him.

'We thought we'd lost you, then.' Brenda smiled at him with laughter in her eyes. 'Poor Reg was beginning to think he'd have to pay the bill.'

'I don't see why he can't do that anyway, it'll let some fresh air into his wallet,' Walsh grumbled.

'Would you like to order now, sir,' the waiter said patiently, in a bored, mock-humble voice.

'Have you both ordered?' Walsh asked.

They nodded.

'I'll have the steak and kidney then, and apple pie. Now we want some drinks, or shall we have a bottle of wine between us?'

'Leave that to you, Chief,' Brenda replied.

'All right, a bottle of your house white, medium dry, then.'

'Thank you, sir. Your meals will be served in just a few minutes. In the mean time, I will bring you the wine.'

The waiter turned away and pushed through the swing

143

doors at the back of the room. Walsh glimpsed white tiles, and a heavy aroma of cooking wafted over to the table.

'What was it I overheard you saying to Gwen last night, Brenda, about you restoring old porcelain and china? That must be very interesting. However did you start doing that?' Walsh asked conversationally.

Brenda blushed slightly. 'Well, it started when I broke one of my mother's vases. It wasn't particularly valuable, but she liked it. I set about gluing it together, using the fast-setting Araldite. I tried to be ever so careful, doing it piece by piece. It took me several hours, and it didn't look too bad when I'd cleaned off the surplus glue, but I didn't like seeing the cracks. However hard you try to fit the pieces together, the joins still show. So I got out some oil paints and had a go with them, running them into the cracks, and I surprised myself. If you looked closely you could still tell that it had been broken, but that was my first, and that's how I got interested. I got some books and read them and started to get the right stuff together. Fortunately, there isn't a shortage of pieces to practise on. You can buy some very nice things from jumble sales or car boot sales, for only a few pence. It keeps me out of mischief, anyway.' She paused as the waiter returned with the wine and poured a sample for Walsh to taste.

'That's fine,' Walsh said, with just the right degree of confidence, and watched as all the glasses were filled. There would be only just enough left in the bottle to top up each glass later on. Walsh saw that Finch's eyes were still on Brenda's face, with a thoughtful look in them too.

'How do you set about matching colours?' Finch asked. 'I would have thought that oil paints would have been too soft to stand up to handling for any length of time.'

'They don't, but that's how I got started. I've learned a lot since then. Colours have to be laid on and fired in descending order, depending on the temperature and the

144

time. The colours for repairs fire at lower temperatures than the original ones,' she replied.

The waiter came back with the food. Walsh found he had an appetite, so he set to with enthusiasm.

'I find people's hobbies quite fascinating,' Walsh mumbled, while still chewing. 'I met a chap once, fusty old fellow, he was. Looking at him you'd have thought his whole world was bound up in paper and figures, but when you got him talking, he became really alive, a different person. He was a collector of "tompions", those things they stick in the muzzle of big guns when they're not being fired. Wealthy captains in the Napoleonic wars often had special ones made with their own crests on. Well, he was an authority, and he knew his naval history as well. Surprising, isn't it? You never know about someone, do you? Like Reg and his archaeology.'

'You've got to remember that the boss here knows more about each of us than we do ourselves, Brenda,' Finch grinned.

'I suppose he does. I hadn't thought about it. Have you done any digging lately, Reg? There aren't many new sites around here, are there?' she asked.

Now he had got them talking, Walsh thought that perhaps he could get back to thinking about the case, but it wasn't possible: the action of eating and the content of the conversation saw to that. Later, maybe.

'Not only that,' Finch was saying, 'there's plenty of field work one can do. It's surprising what one can find, just walking the edges of ploughed fields, especially up on the chalk lands. You get the odd worked flint, fragments of pottery and all sorts of bits and pieces that have dropped through holes in people's pockets over the years. Particularly if you walk the old trackways, and it's quite amazing how interesting that can be, even only using an ordinary Ordnance Survey map. Better with the larger-scale ones, of course.'

Walsh made a start on his apple pie. Plenty of cream, just as he liked it.

He knew what Finch meant, about finding something interesting. He'd once found a fine flint arrowhead on an east-coast beach. Near Walton-on-the-Naze it was, years ago, when he was a kid. There was a special magic about holding something in your hand that was tens of thousands of years old. Yet it had been so neat and well worked that you could have fitted it to a shaft and used it as effectively as if it had just been made. Where it was now he'd no idea. He didn't remember ever throwing it away, and he'd like to look at it again. The edges hadn't been quite straight, they'd curved slightly outwards, like a delta-winged aeroplane, and the barbs were undercut just a fraction. A wicked-looking thing, small though it was. Since then he'd handled many a death-dealing tool, knives, cudgels, pistols, but that arrowhead had been the very first. Maybe that too had been used to kill, although they wouldn't have called it murder then, they'd have said it was war. You could boast about killing in war, but a murderer would be a fool if he shouted about his actions. Usually they became paranoid about keeping it secret, that was often why they killed again. The second time was considered to be easier than the first, and after that a special thrill was supposed to develop, almost an ecstasy at the moment the deed was committed. Ignoring the opinions of future victims, the more the killings continued, the better the chance of the killer making a mistake – or so he had been led to believe by the criminal psychopathologists.

This case didn't seem to follow that theory, though. The number of clues left lying around had been negligible, right from the start. No doubt the forensic boys had the evidence to prove the killer actually was there, or even that he did it, but that Scene-of-Crime stuff was all useless unless he could put forward a suitable suspect out of the several hundred thousand people who lived within a few miles' radius of the city centre. Maybe if they gave him a silver pin to stick in a map, he'd find the killer that way. But killers didn't only kill again just to cover their tracks. Hatred was a powerful motive too. Was there anything about Higgins, Varney and Harrison that could have aroused an over- whelming feeling of hatred in the heart of a killer? Jealousy, in the case of Higgins, because of his mental ability, but surely nothing as far as the other two went? They were nonentities, pawns, weren't they?

'If Harrison was sent to the Stevens' party to make sure that Mrs Higgins wasn't at home when the murderer got there, that suggests the lab director is involved,' Walsh found himself saying out loud.

There was silence for a moment.

'The trouble is, Harrison also had links with Varney, Dubonnet and, as far as we know, Mrs Higgins as well, Chief,' Brenda pointed out.

'True, and we've still got the report on Higgins's stu- dents and the other college staff to go through tonight, as well as the cleaner's son and the others in the group that went to Dubonnet's no-smoking class,' Walsh said. He waved his hand at the waiter, who interpreted the gesture correctly and came over with the bill.

17

'Old Higgins was as cooky as a coot,' Professor Pearson said, appreciatively eyeing Brenda's nylon-clad legs as she sat in the low armchair opposite him.

'How do you mean?' she asked, resisting the desire to try and pull the hem of her grey skirt down to her knee: it wouldn't go any further. She was as prim and proper as it was possible to be, in this outfit.

'It's always a problem when someone tries to get too deep outside his own field. I've known it happen before. Bloody mathematicians turning archaeologists, they get things all mixed up, latch on to some minor aspect, then get their knickers in a twist over it.'

'Is that what Professor Higgins was doing?'

'Yep, bird warning cries and the human subconscious. Well, I ask you, bloody ridiculous, ain't it? Like pronouncing on where human babies come from, after studying fossilized dinosaurs' eggs.'

'I thought he was making the point that the hereditary instincts of humans have many similar characteristics to those of other species,' Brenda said hopefully.

Professor Pearson nodded his head approvingly. 'At least you've tried to understand the gist of his proposition. No, his whole argument falls down on one very simple basis. You've got to compare like with like. Birds and humans? No way. You might as well compare ants and blue whales. Do you see what I mean? If he'd kept within the same species, well then, that'd be a different matter.'

'So you think there's something in what he says, but in a much narrower field?'

Pearson looked wary. 'I didn't actually say that, young lady. Nobody's yet catalogued all the inherited instinct motions, not to my knowledge, but most of them are activated by sight rather than sound. It's your instincts make you jump out of the way of a moving bus, not your conscious mind. If you were deaf and blind when the bus came, you'd be dead as well, see? Now, that's enough of that sort of stuff. Are you interested in antique jewellery, my dear, because I've got a superb collection upstairs. I might even have a piece to spare that'd look really nice round that pretty neck of yours. Come on upstairs, and have a look.'

He advanced on her, all smiles, with hand outstretched, but found that she was already on her feet, announcing how delighted she would have been to see his collection, had not duty required her immediate attention to other matters, elsewhere.

The afternoon was misty, chilly and overcast, a real harbinger of autumn and the coming winter.

Walsh drove through the entrance in the high brick wall at the side of the Headquarters building, to the car-park at the rear. He was fortunate that his seniority entitled him to a named car space: a privilege he appreciated when it was raining, since his spot was close to the rear entrance to the building.

Now, however, Walsh did not go in, but walked back the way he had come, to the road. The exit from the car-park was difficult because the high brick walls restricted visibility to both right and left. It was necessary to creep a car forward slowly until you could see the oncoming traffic, and since the pavement was not very wide the front of the car would just about be on the road by the time you could see round the wall. A large notice gave a warning to those making the journey out. Otherwise the site was ideal: almost in the centre of the city, yet with reasonably good access to all the main roads.

Walsh dug one hand into the pocket of his lightweight waterproof jacket. His other hand carried the inevitable briefcase, which today contained the files of the Higgins, Varney and Harrison cases.

He always took some files home with him. It was impossible to stop his mind working just because the clock said he was off duty, and there was nothing worse than finding that his train of thought required confirmation of some fact or other when he didn't have the information to hand. Sometimes the jigsaw-like pieces of a case came together when he least expected them to, usually when he was doing something else.

He crossed over the road at the traffic lights and headed towards the city.

The round, rosy-faced Professor Hughes welcomed him at the door to his rooms as effusively as he had done the week before.

'Come in, Inspector. The kettle's on the boil,' he said, wandering off to his kitchenette. The room was comfortably warm. A small coal fire glowed in the grate at the far end of the room. Walsh went to warm his hands before it.

Hughes came back with a tray.

'You've found the fire, I see. Shouldn't really have it, it's not that cold today, but I like pampering myself, and it's a bit gloomy outside. A bit of what you fancy does you good, they say. Not that I care much what they say, these days. Makes the room nice and cosy, doesn't it? Come and have your coffee. You're looking a bit tired, if you don't mind my saying so.' Hughes handed Walsh a cup and pulled another of the high, leather-upholstered chairs over to the fireplace.

'There we are, now we can talk. How's it all going? I hear

150

things have got more complicated than they were, with two more bodies. Has that made things easier or worse?'

Walsh didn't mind talking to this clever, needle-sharp old man, who obviously had some level of security rating with the unknown ministry department. Nevertheless, he confined his outline sketch of the case to generalities, then had the feeling that this wise old Professor was filling in the gaps with no problem at all.

Hughes leaned back in his chair. 'Fascinating. You're a lucky man in many ways, you know. You live through the best type of Agatha Christie's stories, but in real life. Problem-solving is the optimum use of mental activity and the sole reason for man's present state of civilization, such as it is. I envy you, although I'm sure I would quickly lose interest in the routine collection and verification of the facts that you need before you can sit down somewhere, warm and comfortable, and set about solving your case.' Hughes reached over to put down his empty cup. 'Unfortunately, I have little to add to what I've already told you concerning others working in the same area as Higgins's researches. That chap in Scotland has been on a lecture tour in the States for the past few weeks and the German hasn't left Düsseldorf, I can assure you of that. Frankly, I feel this line of inquiry leads nowhere. All those who might have wanted to steal Higgins's work and announce it as their own appear to have been openly and publicly active, well away from the scene of the crime. But these other murders? I'm assuming that you do not accept that Varney's and Harrison's deaths are coincidences. They suggest to me that the thief is local, and has remained local.' Hughes paused for a moment, concerned in case Walsh was either bored or offended by his long speech. In fact, although Walsh was feeling physically tired, he found his mind was being stimulated by Hughes's lecture-like conversation.

Hughes carried on. 'These other killings are to cover his tracks, I would have thought. So, unless you consider that the motive was to obtain access to poor Higgins's personal wealth, you have a problem deciding precisely what the thief hopes to gain from possession of the device. Revenge, hatred – of course they have to be taken into account, although generally, I understand, they form a low proportion of the motives for murder. What then does the killer have in mind? He can't publish the results and gain wealth or recognition. It's very unlikely that a freelance espionage man would be local, and still hanging about, after he'd got what he wanted. I've thought about security, about all these nuclear bases we've got round here. That machine is pretty potent even if its range is short, but it's not just a matter of getting on to those sites. That's probably not very difficult for a determined person, even if security is much tighter where the bombs or aircraft are actually kept on a base than it is at the main gates. What do you do with a bomb if you do get one? They're not exactly the size of a suitcase, are they? And you'd need a detonator,' Hughes observed.

Walsh rubbed his chin thoughtfully. It was all very well sitting there playing armchair detectives. He was the one that had the responsibility for finding and verifying the facts. Even at this moment there were dozens of people working on the case, checking alibis, searching through records, verifying statements, let alone all those in forensic, probing chemically for clues.

'It's possible, but it implies some international link-up: not much point otherwise. Besides, I wouldn't have thought that there were signs of extremely good planning, not if the last two murders were needed to cover tracks. Real professionals wouldn't have left any tracks,' Walsh added.

'Very true, my boy, if it was just the professionals. It might not be quite the same if one of the international terrorist organizations were involved. Their planning might not be as ruthless as their determination to succeed.'

152

Walsh felt a twinge of mental panic. Against world-wide terrorist networks, with all their erratic resources, he was going to be well and truly out of his depth. Was Hughes trying to confuse him? A glance at the expression on his face merely showed a look of deep concern and thoughtfulness. 'Possibly you're right,' he said, 'but to be practical, there does seem to be a local connection running through all the cases. Are you sure you can't think of anyone else in the University, here, or anyone who might be interested in the commercial aspects, whatever they might be, instead of just the academic prestige?' Walsh asked.

'I'm afraid not,' Hughes replied. 'As I've said, the commercial possibilities are pretty negligible, in this country anyway. The thing would undoubtedly be banned. The possible infringement of human liberties would most certainly take precedence over any case for public order control. Military purposes under a top-security classification? Well, that's a different story entirely. Maybe the motive of the person you are after is a simple one, petty larceny. Lots of small cash robberies, and that sort of thing. Like you've had out in the villages.'

Walsh pricked his ears up at that. He'd not mentioned them, so if Hughes knew about them the information must have been fed back via Hutchinson.

'Of all the options, that's the one I hope it turns out to be, but I'm afraid there's more ruthlessness in this than the run-of-the-mill petty thief employs. We shall see what we shall see,' Walsh remarked philosophically. He certainly wasn't a fatalist, but the comment served as a means of bringing the conversation to a suitable conclusion.

He left the elegant comfort of the college.

Academics like Hughes and Higgins knew a thing or two about thinking, and the working of the brain. He remembered how he had felt while sitting in that deep, leather-covered chair, in Higgins's study, with that weird feeling of floating, and Marion Dubonnet's deep blue eyes foremost in his mind. Then he'd had the ability to think freely. It wasn't quite the same in the chair in Hughes's rooms, but if he'd been on his own, maybe that clear-headed thinking would have occurred again. There might be enough facts lurking in the recesses of his mind to solve the problem. Was that all it needed? A comfortable chair, peace, and the time to think? It was certainly an interesting proposition; maybe a paper ought to be written on the subject, if one hadn't been already. He thought of his own office – basic, spartan, a work place, not much of a thinking room. Surely the Eastern meditators didn't need such luxuries? Possibly Hughes and Higgins were displaying the decadence of European civilization by wallowing in such comfort. Mind over matter was possible anywhere, at any time: that's what the ancient philosophers thought.

He walked slowly back to Headquarters.

There was time to take his coat into his office and to visit the cloakroom before making his way up to see the C.C.

Naturally, the C.C. had a much bigger and better furnished office than his own, but it certainly didn't approach the style or atmosphere of Hughes's room. Why was he so concerned about comfort? Was he just tired or was his subconscious telling him that if it had the right conditions it would pin down a murderer for him? Whatever it was, it needed to be put to one side while he was with the C.C. In any interview, even a short briefing session like this, the older man was sharp, shrewd, quick to the point, and hard with his judgements too, if he thought the matter warranted it.

'Hello, Sidney. How's things going? Are you getting anywhere?' the C.C. asked in greeting.

Walsh set out, very briefly, the various possibilities that he and his team had discussed, and the further action that he had set in motion. It was really only a matter of courtesy to tell the C.C. about the use of surveillance teams on Mrs Higgins, her son's wife, Mrs Dubonnet, the lab director, and Holmes and Mrs Mannering, as well as the obtaining of private financial information, if for no other reason than to prevent him from saying later that he didn't know about them.

The C.C. grunted his approval.

'You seem to have things under control, as much as can be reasonably expected. Of course I want miracles, but I'm not daft. Just keep things moving forward, steady like, and you'll get there in the end. How did you get on with friend Hughes this afternoon?'

'He didn't have anything to add to what we already knew, but it wasn't a waste of time talking to him. He's got a hell of a brain, and knew things he could only have learned through Hutchinson, at that government department. He worried me a bit when he talked about organized crime and terrorist activities on an international level, even though the IRA watchers in London don't know of any activity in our area. He'd even been thinking of raids on military bases and installations, using Higgins's machine. I hope those London people appreciate the seriousness of the problem, if it is espionage.'

The C.C. looked thoughtful. He was not one who would fail to give his full support to his staff, if he thought it was needed. Maybe it was, in this case.

'As long as you keep these things in mind, you should carry on as you are. After all, we've got the security services involved. For the time being we're doing the right thing. You'd better brief me again tomorrow. I want to be kept up to date on this case.'

Walsh walked slowly back to his office.

He made himself pick up the reports of yesterday evening's interviews at the riverside pub and its neighbouring houses. He wasn't surprised that there was nothing in them: that would have been too much to expect. No one had seen Harrison drive into the car-park or whom he'd met there. The files were sectionalized, of course; the

155

Dubonnet one was getting thicker. He read it through again. It was almost impossible to believe that she could have murdered in cold blood, yet his training warned him otherwise. Her alibi on the night her husband had died still needed verification, but those deep blue eyes that he kept visualizing were mighty powerful in a strange way. Were they the reason why he kept harking back to that comfortable thinker's chair in Higgins's study?

The phone rang.

'There's someone wants a word with you, sir, but won't give a name.'

'Male or female?'

'Difficult to say, sir. Could be a man trying to sound like a woman, or the other way round. Shall I put the caller through, sir?'

'Do that.'

The phone clicked, and there was a moment's silence after Walsh had announced himself; then he heard the dialling tone.

He looked at his watch – gone eight already. Time for a break.

He put the files back into his case and left a note for Finch and Brenda on his desk. He also rang the duty sergeant and told him he'd be back at nine.

The sky was still overcast and it was quite dark. A misty drizzle fell. He wiped the car windows before getting in. Gwen would knock him up a meal of some sort in no time at all, then he could get back here, to see the other two. He'd try to make sure that this evening's meeting didn't go on too long. He still had not fully recovered from the loss of sleep he'd suffered during the past two days, even after having stayed in bed most of that morning.

With headlights dipped and wipers going, he drove out of the car-park, slipping the clutch to creep slowly forward through the entrance in the high walls. The driver's window was already covered with rain drops, so he wound it down.

He wanted to turn left so he only needed to wait for a gap in the traffic from the right. There were plenty of cars still about, but there was only one pedestrian, coming towards him. His car was now straddling the pavement, so that person would have to wait. Tough. There was a gap coming up. What was that person up to? It was difficult to see clearly, the light was from behind. Was he opening his coat? Not a flasher, not here, outside the police station, on a night like this, surely?

A car went the other way. It's lights momentarily showed a glimpse of a box in the person's hands.

A black box, and it was being aimed at him.

There was no time to think, instant fear blocked his thoughts anyway, but his survival instincts were active. His right foot went down on the accelerator and his left foot abruptly raised the clutch. The powerful, two litre car leapt forward violently, slamming his head back on to the rest. His hands scrabbled to turn the wheel, then they raised themselves to cover his ears.

An intense cacophony of awful sounds bored their way through his skull and into his head, echoing round and round. A vision of a red, devilish face with frightful blazing eyes and bared, vicious teeth appeared right in front of him. His teeth gritted and the palms of each hand pressed his ears painfully against his skull. He sensed the car rocking and swaying. The pain in his head eased a little, but there were other noises. It was the engine that was screaming, but those other sounds were him, screaming just as loud. There was a crashing explosion, he jerked forward against his seat belt, then blackness, and nothing.

18

A faint light appeared in the darkness, high up and a long way off. Reluctantly, Walsh's mind struggled slowly towards it. No thoughts existed and time was part of unreality. After a while, forms and shapes appeared to move within the lighted area and his curiosity made moves to identify them, forcing his eyes to try and focus. The forms gradually became blurred faces. None of them he knew. The rest of the white area turned out to be a ceiling. He became conscious of sounds, hollow and distant, like echoes from a rocky hillside, causing him to wince in anticipation of pain, but there was no pain, only a dull ache. Now he'd realized that an ache was there, it spread, round behind his eyes and temples until it encompassed the whole of his head. Gradually more aches formed themselves in other parts of his body as his sense of feeling returned. It wasn't pleasant, although it was bearable.

He moved his hands to try and push downwards, to raise his head and shoulders. Other hands came to help him and to pile soft cool pillows behind his head.

He turned his head to thank those who'd helped, but only a peculiar croaking sound came from his mouth.

Here was a face he knew. What was her name?

'Hello, Chief, it's Brenda. How are you feeling?'

His hands raised themselves to cover his ears. 'Not so loud, don't shout,' he managed to whisper.

'He's talking, and I think he knows me,' the voice of Brenda was heard to say to someone else.

'He's damned lucky,' a male voice said.

Walsh ignored them. He was conscious of his surroundings now. This room was in a hospital, and he was in a single bed. There were lots of pipes and gadgets about, fortunately not in use.

The doctor leaned over him and shone a tiny beam of light into his eyes and felt his pulse. 'Looks promising. Don't talk to him unless he wants you to. I'll tell his wife that he's regained consciousness,' the man said in a low voice.

Walsh was content to lie quietly.

Through the window came weak sunlight, just enough to create faint shadows on the windowsill. The aches in his head receded a little, then Gwen came in.

He smiled with pleasure at the sight of her. It seemed such a long while since he had last gazed on her features. His wife was still a beauty to him. It was a pity she had such a worried expression on her face.

'Hello, love. Where've you been?' he asked softly.

Gwen's bottom lip trapped itself between her teeth, but even so it still managed to tremble. She bent and kissed his cheek, blinking back tears of relief. 'I've been downstairs having a cup of coffee. How are you feeling?' she whispered.

'Me? I'm fine. I'm not sure yet what I'm doing here, but no doubt someone will tell me eventually. I've got a lot to do, but I can't recall what, at the moment, and I've got a bit of a headache. I feel as though I've been kicked about a bit. I haven't been playing rugby again, have I?' Memories of a short jinking run on soft muddy turf, and no support, no one to pass to, a wall of striped jerseys in front, then a torn, bleeding left ear and two broken ribs.

'No, darling, you haven't played rugby for years. You've

been in a car accident, that's all,' Gwen informed him, taking his hand into hers.

'Oh dear, sorry about that. I didn't hurt anyone, did I?' he asked.

'No, dear, you were very lucky.'

'Good, no need to report it then.' That was satisfactory news. There was someone else there. It was rude to ignore her. 'And you, Brenda, are you well?' he asked.

'I'm fine, Chief. I got back to HQ in time to see them pulling you out from the front of a red double-decker bus,' she replied.

HQ? So there was more to life than this room. He frowned as the memories came flooding back, and it became necessary to sit himself more upright.

'I can manage, thanks. I was coming home, love . . .' He rubbed his hand over his forehead in an effort to force his brain to think.

'Take it easy, darling, there's no hurry,' Gwen told him anxiously.

'No, I'm all right, but there's something important. As I was coming out of the car-park, someone was walking towards me. It was difficult to see, what with the rain and the lights, but there was a black box. I must have panicked, because I don't remember much else, except the pain in my head. That was after I'd moved off, so it must have come from the box, but it wasn't like those tests of Hutchinson's. I didn't feel a thing then. This whammed into my ears, and hurt, nearly drove me mad. Frankly I don't want to try and remember it. It wasn't pleasant.' Walsh closed his eyes.

He heard the sound of someone using the telephone that stood on the table by the window.

'Detective Constable Phipps. I'm phoning from Addenbrookes Hospital. Put me through to the Chief Constable, please,' he heard Brenda's voice say. 'Good morning, sir. The Inspector's regained conciousness. Yes, he's talking all right. There was someone with a black box outside, got him

160

as he drove out of the car-park. Yes, I know, but this was different, much louder, and painful as well, nearly drove him mad. I was thinking, sir, Hutchinson said that Higgins had built in a safety limit circuit into his machine. Yes, that's right, sir. I think someone's overridden it, and knows what effect it has, too.'

Walsh opened his eyes and turned his head. 'Let me speak to him, Brenda.' His voice sounded harsh and husky, not at all like his own.

'Hold on a minute, sir. He wants to talk to you himself.' She came over to the bed and handed the receiver to Walsh.

'Hello there. Yes, I'm a bit groggy still, but I'm feeling better all the time. That's right. Right outside HQ. As soon as I realized, I went off like a bat out of hell, but not fast enough apparently. No, I don't want anyone else to take over. There's nothing broken as far as I can tell. Yes, I'll take things easy for the rest of the day. No doubt I'll be as right as rain in the morning. All right, good idea. I'll have someone drive me around for a day or two. I want to see Finch and Brenda, to find out what's been going on. What's that? You've got to mess up our surveillance roster? Well, if you need the men that bad, of course. I'll ring you this evening, if you like. Will you be at home, or shall we leave it till tomorrow? Right then. Yes, I will. Goodbye.' He handed the phone back to Brenda.

'What's all this about a black box, Sidney? Have you got someone gunning for you? Because if you have, I want to know about it,' Gwen said firmly.

'What's that, love? The black box? It fires sound pulses, knocks the mind out for a while. Better than being shot with a gun. Yes, I suppose someone was after me. Why, I haven't worked out yet, but if I know the Chief Constable, he's pulled off my late-night surveillance teams and I bet at least some of them will be watching over us tonight. Right, Brenda?' Walsh replied.

Brenda grinned. 'I don't suppose he's too pleased about

161

anyone having a go at you, and to give him his due, he wouldn't believe that there hadn't been a good reason why you smashed your car up. I shouldn't think there's anything for you to worry about, Mrs Walsh.'

'Gwen, if you don't mind Brenda, I'm not in the police force. I'm just an innocent bystander, who doesn't want her man to get injured or maimed,' she said bitterly.

There was an embarrassed silence.

'I'll tell you what I want, Gwen. I want you to drive me home. I suppose my clothes are somewhere round here?' Walsh asked.

'You'd have to see the doctor first, dear. Brenda, see if you can find him while I sit on Superman here. You've had a massive shock to your system. You've got to rest and take things easy. Maybe they'll want to keep you in for observation.'

Walsh lay back, a slight smile on his face. Gwen had looked as though she was going to have a tantrum. It wasn't surprising, really; she had probably been here all last night as well, worrying about him.

The young doctor pushed the door open, followed by Brenda. 'You want to get up and go, do you? Well, how are you feeling? If you can walk all right, I'll let you go. If you can't, I won't. Come on, let's see.' He pulled the bed covers back.

Walsh swung his legs off the bed, feeling highly embarrassed in the flimsy back-to-front white gown he found that he was wearing, and pushed himself upright. The room started to swing, but he focused his eyes firmly on the window catch, waited a moment, then took some steps round the room.

'There you are,' he grunted triumphantly. 'Fit as a fiddle.'

The doctor grinned. 'You take things easy for a day or two, Inspector. If there's any problem, don't be daft, you come straight back here. Your body is all in one piece, but your brain's been badly shaken up. Keep your eye on him, Mrs Walsh, won't you?'

'Brenda,' Gwen said, 'I'm not going to let him go out once I get him home, so if you and Reg want to see him, you'll have to come round. Any time, it doesn't matter.'

'I understand. Shall we say about four? I'm sure that'll be all right with Reg. See you later, Chief,' she replied.

Parked down the road, in an unmarked patrol car, someone was watching the aproaches to the Walsh house: a visible sign of the Chief Constable's determination to ensure that no third party had an easy opportunity to shorten the life expectancy of a valued member of his team.

When Reginald Finch turned into the road, he wisely slowed down as he passed that car and raised his hand slightly in acknowledgement, allowing the watcher to see him and his passenger clearly, before going on to park outside Walsh's house.

His ring on the front door bell roused the two sleepers inside.

'Come on in, both of you,' Gwen said, as she opened the door. 'Sidney's in the sitting-room. We've been having forty winks. Go in. I'll make some coffee. Good heavens look at the time, I'd better get some food as well.'

Brenda led the way into the sitting-room. It was a little too warm, she thought.

'Hello, Chief,' she said cheerily, as she flicked on the lights. Walsh's face seemed more relaxed than when she had seen him earlier in the day, and there was more colour in his cheeks.

He blinked up at them, and wriggled himself more up-right in his chair. 'Come on in, and sit yourselves down. Draw the curtains, Reg, if you don't mind,' he said, stifling a yawn.

Finch looked doubtful. It wasn't usual to see the boss in

163

comfortable, creaseless corduroys and sweater; normally he wore a suit and tie, as befitted his status. Now, in some ways, he looked younger, but there were deeper lines round the eyes and down the cheeks.

'Do you feel up to talking, boss, or shall we leave it until tomorrow?' he asked, patting the curtain folds into order.

'I want to get up to date with what's going on, Reg. Anyway, I'm feeling a lot better now. Pass me my briefcase, please. Now, how have you been getting on?' he asked.

Brenda spoke first. 'We've set up the investigation into the personal finances of everyone on our list. As usual, the banks wouldn't play ball without being approached directly, so Reg and I split them between us. That's what we were doing yesterday afternoon. I've added to the reports on Higgins's son's wife. She's been involved in a few scuffles on left-wing rallies and marches, but never bad enough to result in prosecutions. Packstone's lot are still going through the stuff they took from Higgins's and Varney's places, and from Harrison's body, trying to find some common factor, further report tomorrow. Mrs Higgins did go out to friends in Sawston the night Harrison was killed, and arrived when she said, but there was still time for her to do it after she left, so she's not out of it yet. Same with the lab director, Holmes and Mrs Mannering, and Jim Byatt.'

Gwen came in with a tray of cups and plates. 'Here you are, help yourselves,' she said, putting the tray down on one of the low tables. 'There's toasted cheese sandwiches, apple pies and coconut cookies. That should keep the wolf from the door for a while. Here's your coffee, darling.' She handed him a cup. 'I've things to do in the kitchen, so I'll get on.'

'What about Dubonnet?' Walsh asked.

'Yes, Chief, she's under daytime surveillance, as are Mrs Higgins and the lab director,' Brenda replied. 'I've brought some of the other reports that you haven't seen yet. They're all negative, or confirmatory. Nothing special.'

'I spoke to Hutchinson this afternoon,' Finch added, 'and explained the effect Higgins's machine had on you. He agrees that the volume override's been bypassed. It's now an extremely dangerous weapon, at short range. Likely to cause permanent madness. He thinks you're damned lucky. The back of your car acted as a muffle, and accelerating away as quickly as you did saved your reason, boss,' Finch continued seriously.

'Such as it is,' Walsh mumbled, smiling.

'Can you remember any more about the person carrying the box now, Chief?' Brenda asked.

'Not really. The light was coming from behind, so it was just a silhouette, and the shape was all bundled up and bulky. I'm almost certain there was a hat or a hood. The box was under a coat or maybe a cloak, that's why I got away, you know, because of that fumbling with the coat. I panicked I suppose. I can't even recall an impression of size, the image just seems to float in my mind, so I can't say whether the figure was short or tall, fat or thin.'

Brenda took a surreptitious look at her watch. They had been there too long already; there was nothing that couldn't wait till the morning. They should get away soon. 'But why would whoever-it-is take such a risk as to try and nobble you, Chief? How would anyone know you were still in HQ, for starters?' she demanded.

'There was a phone call a little earlier, before I went out. Rang off when it was put through. I suppose that was it. As to why, if we knew that, we'd probably know the killer.'

'Perhaps someone thinks we're nearly on to them, boss, and is getting scared.'

Walsh suddenly jerked himself upright. 'Hell fire, I've just thought. That machine might have been tested on someone else, before it was used on me. You two had better

165

get checking the hospitals and surgeries, and find out. We might get a lead that way.'

'OK, Chief, and if there's nothing else, we'll be getting along. If anything crops up tonight we can brief you in the morning, before you see the Chief Constable,' she said, rising to her feet and glaring a challenge to Finch. They'd been there quite long enough. The Chief really wasn't a well man.

'All right, you two cut along. I'll see you in the morning.' Walsh started to get up.

'No, you stay there, boss. We can see ourselves out,' Finch added anxiously.

Walsh just raised a hand instead – if they wanted to pamper him, let them get on with it.

He heard goodbyes being called out to Gwen, the front door slamming and the sound of Finch's car being started.

It was funny. From the sounds you heard, you could visualize in your mind what was actually happening outside. His head rested back into the softness of the chair and his feet made an effort to hook the stool closer. Yes, in his mind he could picture those two walking down the drive. Finch would have opened the passenger door for Brenda, and then have walked round the car to get in himelf. The darkness and the faint light from the street lamps, the hazy mistiness from the fine drizzle: it was almost as though he was looking out of the window.

The sound of the car engine receded into the distance, and all was peace and quiet. He could hear only the faint humming of the flames of the gas fire. He felt a bit light-headed, much as he had when he had sat in Higgins's leather armchair, the one in his study.

What was in the mind of the killer? Higgins's death might have been prompted by panic at being disturbed. Varney's, if he was blackmailing or threatening the killer, might have been the result of anger, but Harrison was killed in cold

166

blood, no doubt about that. The attack on himself, too – that was done in cold blood. Making him mad would be just as effective as killing him. But why? Obviously, even if he didn't know it, he was brushing up too close for someone's peace of mind. That didn't narrow the field much; they were working on a lot of people at the same time. One of them was getting scared, another pointer to the theory of it being someone local. On the other hand, there could be another reason, couldn't there? The attack on himself could be a delaying tactic, to give someone time to do something. But what?

His brain must have decided that he should rest, because he fell asleep again.

It was just before nine when Gwen opened the door and woke him. Several times she had peeped in and decided not to disturb him.

'Oh, you're awake again, are you? I hope you're not going to find you can't sleep when we go to bed. Can I get you anything? Or would you like to watch the news?' She switched the television on, and sat down herself.

The face of the newscaster was serious. 'This is the first time the conference has been back to Brighton since the IRA bombing of four years ago. The security measures are the most stringent ever. The cost is reported to be in the region of one and a half million pounds. A Royal Navy mine-sweeper is stationed out at sea, directly opposite the hotel. A report from our man at the conference.'

Another face, another voice. 'Precautions this year are tighter than ever before. The security staff are convinced that no unauthorized persons can gain entry into the hotel where the Prime Minister and most of the Cabinet will be staying tonight, and for each night of the conference.'

Walsh smiled grimly to himself. There would be little difficulty for someone with a Higgins machine in their hands. His mind repeated those words again, and suddenly they meant something. He leapt to his feet, nearly tripping over the stool.

'Oh my God,' he muttered, as he ran for the telephone.

19

'You must be out of your tiny mind, Sidney. No one could get within a hundred yards of that place without being jumped on. Are you all right? Maybe you should have stayed in hospital another night.' The C.C.'s booming tones became more soothing at the end, as if to calm down an upset child.

'For Christ's sake, listen. Anyone with that machine could walk through any cordon, like a hot knife through butter. Of course I'm not a hundred per cent sure that's what the killer's got in mind. What I'm saying is that we can't afford to take the chance. Got it?' Walsh was almost shouting.

'All right, all right, Sidney, calm down. I can see what you're driving at. Precautionary measures, eh? You haven't got any firm reasons to back it up, have you?' the C.C. asked in a more reasonable tone of voice.

'We've got suspects that are left-wing, anti-establishment and hold a grudge against the government. Even without them we don't know that it's not the IRA who've got the damned thing. I'll say it again. We've got no choice. We've got to take it seriously. If someone gets in that place, think of what could happen and the repercussions. All they've got to do is turn the volume up, walk around a few floors and a whole government's gone mad. There'd be chaos, not only here, but internationally. Every government in the world is just as vulnerable, at some time or other. You must see that.'

'Yes, Sidney, I do. It's preposterous, but you're right. What do you suggest we do?'

'We are the only people who know what we're looking for, and we've got a small immune team, so we've got to get down there, now, tonight, and cover that place, until Hutchinson can do the same tests on the people down there as he did up here. Now, what I want is this.' Walsh was calmer now, as his mind wrestled with the problem. 'Two, no, three fast patrol cars to take all the immune lot and me to Brighton. I can't see us getting down there until half one in the morning, maybe two, depends on the traffic. What you've got to do, sir, is to pave the way for us. We can't just draw up outside and walk in – think of all the possibilities of misunderstandings and delays. You'll have to get on to the Home Secretary or someone else in authority, and I want one of the Sussex cars to escort us right to the front door. Get one of the top dogs down there to meet us outside. Someone who can take us straight in, without any fuss. You've got to organize that, you're the only one with the necessary clout to put that together in the time we've got. Right?'

'Bloody hell fire, you don't ask much, do you? All right! All right! God knows what'll happen to our reputations.'

'I don't care a sod. We'll be doing the right thing, that's all I care about. We'd best be armed, too, I think. You'd better authorize the armoury as well,' Walsh interrupted impatiently.

'What the hell are you waiting for, then? Get a move on. I'll be in touch with you on your car radio. Er, best of luck, Sidney.'

The phone went dead.

Walsh dialled HQ, and barked out instructions to the harassed duty officer.

He turned away, feeling dizzy, to get himself ready, and

170

found an anxious Gwen by his side holding up a light waterproof jacket for him to slide his arms into the sleeves. His wallet, in which he kept cash and his identity card and documents, lay ready for him on the table.

He smiled, and put his arms round her, his fingers twisting themselves caressingly in her hair, as his lips met hers.

The front door bell rang.

It was Gwen that pushed him away and went to open it. The young driver of the unmarked patrol car stood there grinning.

'Taxi, sir.' His face was boyish and the grin infectious.

Gwen turned back to grasp her husband's hand as he slipped the wallet into his pocket. Pipe, tobacco and lighter went in the wide pockets.

'Take care, dear,' she said softly, resisting the temptation to say that he shouldn't be going out.

'Don't worry, love. There's no danger tonight, not for me, anyway,' he said hopefully. 'I'll ring you when we get there, if you like, but you ought to be in bed and asleep by then.'

'Do it anyway. I'll rest better, knowing you're all right,' she replied, her eyes looking just a little watery.

He nodded. 'Come on, then, taxi driver,' he said, and strode off, not looking back.

'You were quick,' Walsh grunted, as he sat down in the passenger seat and fumbled with the seat belt.

'Well, I've been parked down the road for the last hour or so, keeping an eye on your place,' came the reply, as the driver moved up the gears, slickly, racing style.

So, the C.C. had set up a watch over him.

Now there was just this business to get over, and then things could return to normal. Not only that, once he'd wound this case up he'd take some leave. He and Gwen could get away to the sun somewhere. Just the thought made him feel more cheerful than he'd felt for a long time now. He thought about using the car radio to find out how things were progressing, but he decided against it. His orders had been quite precise and they would be carried out. He'd only end up blocking an incoming line. In any case, this young fellow was driving well, another five minutes and they would be there.

There was plenty of bustle in the briefing room, where everyone was collecting. The duty sergeant met him at the door.

'Just a few more minutes, sir, and they'll all be here. I've got two cars ready, the third's just filling up with petrol. It won't be long. The drivers are all fresh, they haven't been out for more than an hour or so. I've got to log them out, though, sir. Where are you taking them?' he asked.

'Brighton. Now, that young fellow that brought me in, send him back where he was, keeping an eye on my place. When he gets there I want you to ring my wife, tell her we're on our way, or something, just to make sure nothing has happened since I left. OK?'

The duty sergeant nodded and moved away as Brenda came over, her hair in some disorder as though she'd dressed in a hurry. Blue jeans, sweater and quilted body warmer, very feminine, in spite of her garb. 'I was just going to have an early night, Chief. We're only waiting for Joe Mason to be brought in. They had to go and fetch him. They couldn't get him on the phone for some reason. What's up, Chief, are we going to pick someone up? I've even been given a pistol.' She sounded excited. The Browning automatic looked more like a cannon in her small hand.

Walsh shook his head.

Joe Mason appeared in the doorway, his face looking mystified by all the activity. Walsh grasped his shoulder and drew him into the room.

'Now, listen, all of you,' he said loudly.

There was immediate silence, as they turned to face him.

172

Joe Mason and the other deaf man fiddled with their hearing aids.

'You remember those tests you had, when the man came with that small black box?' Heads nodded. 'Well, it's just possible that there's one of those gadgets down in Brighton. We're going down there now, to provide an extra security screen during the night, that's all. Nothing to panic about. Don't worry about your homes. I know you couldn't tell your folk what you were up to, but the duty sergeant will handle all that when we've gone. We should be back late tomorrow morning. Now, Joe and Brenda will come with me in the first car, the rest of you can sort yourselves out in the other two. Right, let's go. Now, Sergeant, there's something else you've got to do,' he said, taking the duty sergeant by the elbow and drawing him to one side. 'You must get all our identity details wired down to Sussex. I don't want to take any chance of there being a mix-up. Ring the C.C. and tell him what you've done. He'll make sure that the right people pick them up at the other end. Then get hold of Finch. I want the people on this list brought into HQ. Make up your own reasons, I don't care what they are, but I want them kept here all night, got it?'

He tore out a sheet from his notebook and handed it to the sergeant, then hurried after the others, out to the waiting cars.

The sergeant glanced down at the list and frowned. All-night questioning, that spelt trouble and hassle, as if there hadn't been enough already on this shift. Well, bloody Finch could take some of the sweat. He turned on his heels, grumbling to himself, to set things in motion.

Walsh found the other two waiting outside the car. He pulled open the offside rear door.

'You in the front, Joe,' he mouthed as he got in.

The car moved forward to the exit between the high walls. Walsh looked curiously out of the window as the car paused, momentarily, but the wall obscured his view of

173

where the figure with the black box had been. Was it only last night? The car accelerated away, with all the smoothness and power of its eight cylinders. The fleeting glimpse through the window to his right brought back no more memories, and he was thankful for that.

It had obviously stopped raining some time back, because the roads were almost dry now. The clouds must be breaking up, because the sky was lighter, not black and heavy as it had been the previous evening.

He settled back into the plush upholstery, pulled down the centre arm squab and fastened the rear seat belt. Now he could relax a few of his aching muscles. He had done all he could for the time being. No doubt his brain would want to waste its time going over and over the same things again, but there wasn't a lot he could do about that. There really was nothing more he could do until they got to Brighton. It was probably all a waste of time, anyway.

What odds would a bookie give on a rank outside chance like this? Fifty to one? More like a hundred to one. He mustn't forget that he was in the middle of a triple murder inquiry: but that had been a frightening vision he'd had when that television programme came on, of what a determined person might do with that damned black box.

It would be the terrorists' coup of the century, of any century, probably; the greatest coup that had ever been. There would be unheard-of opportunities for unruly elements to create the break-up of established law and order. The fear that would be created in other governments throughout the world could easily verge on panic, putting such a sudden strain on security organizations that they would be bound to weaken, if not to break altogether. Not a happy picture. Who, on his suspect list, might be planning that sort of thing? They'd earn fame, of a sort, whatever happened. They'd be like Guy Fawkes, in the history books, for certain.

He turned his head to look back out of the window. They

174

were on the M11 now. The other two cars were keeping close, but not too close. The drivers were staying in the outside lane, and going fast. He looked forward, leaning over to his left to peer round the driver's seat. There were cars up in front. He saw the driver flash his headlights and set the blue light on the roof going. It reflected from the bonnet, not that he could actually see the bonnet, only the flicker of blue as the light flashed. The cars in front quickly sorted themselves out. No doubt the drivers who had been going over the speed limit were even now crossing their fingers, their hearts beating faster at the thought of being caught, especially those previous offenders for whom one more conviction would result in a disqualification. Still, they would have luck on their side tonight. They might wonder at the purpose of the high-speed convoy, but they'd never guess.

He caught sight of the digital clock at the far end of the dashboard. It was well past eleven. It was surprisng how long it had taken to get this far, yet everything had seemed to go so quickly and smoothly.

He felt in his pocket for his pipe. He hadn't smoked at all that day, he just hadn't felt like it; now it would be soothing and relaxing. He reached forward to the ashtray to scrape the old dottle from the bowl, with a key on his key-ring. The one he used was the ignition key from his car. Normally he avoided using that in case some of the tar gathered in the groove of the key and got left in the lock and eventually jammed it, but he'd never drive that car again: it was a write-off.

There was very little light for him to see what he was doing. It didn't matter – pipe-filling was a routine that was almost second nature to him. He lit up, breathing in the fumes contentedly.

'M25 soon,' he said to Brenda.

For a woman, she had remained remarkably quiet so far.

'The only problems will be at the Dartford tunnel and in

175

Brighton itself, Chief, if we're going to get any. Have you got any idea who we might find down there?' she asked, implying that she didn't believe that they were just taking precautionary measures, and that in some way he'd worked it all out.

'Yes, I rather think I have,' he heard himself say.

Surprising, that. Now when had he worked that out? Until that moment he hadn't even realized that he had come to a conclusion. By logical reasoning, that's how he knew, but it would need the forensic team to come up with the detailed evidence necessary to obtain a judgement in court. Most of the dust and particles collected from the scenes of the crimes would be useless, but once he'd pointed a finger, with all the drama of an old-fashioned witch doctor, then the Scene-of-Crime team would tear into the clothes, shoes and living area, taking impossibly minute samples, then spend hours and hours on microscopic analysis, making comparisons with samples taken from where the crimes had been committed. It was almost impossible for contacts between surfaces not to leave some detectable trace. Applied science had developed at a tremendous rate during the years that Walsh had been involved in the detection of crime, so much so that he would be the first to admit that nowadays he only had an appreciation of the techniques, rather than an understanding of them all.

'Who is it, Chief?' Brenda asked.

Walsh felt too weary to go into all the whys and wherefores such a discussion would entail. Not only that, he still had some thinking to do before they got down to the Grand Hotel. He had to put himself into the killer's mind, and try and work out what the plan of operation would be, and how it would be carried out.

Perhaps his reply of, 'Not just now,' may have sounded rude, but he hadn't intended it to be so.

It started drizzling again just before the Dartford tunnel.

On the other side of the Thames, it was raining. A few moments later, it was sheeting down.

The pace slowed, the driver had to have the wipers going at fast speed. Then they were down to a crawl, all the lanes becoming congested and, eventually, blocked. The driver had his left indicator and blue light on, forcing a passage through the middle and inside lanes, on to the hard shoulder.

'We'll probably be all right once we're past the Dover traffic, sir,' the driver said over his shoulder, his eyes peering intently forward.

They hadn't gone far when they came up to an accident. Two lorries and three crumpled cars lay strewn across the motorway. The rain streamed down; silver streaks in the bright headlights.

A police officer in a bright orange coat swung round angrily as the white Rover nosed forward on the hard shoulder; then he saw the flashing lights and ran over. The driver's electric window slid down. Walsh could see other members of the crews of two patrol cars on the scene, working frantically at the remains of a car caught up under the rear end of one of the lorries.

'Sorry, mate. We've got to go through,' the driver said. The other man didn't argue: it wasn't worth it on a night like this. He turned and ran over towards the outside lane, beckoning them to follow. Then he stopped and pointed at a narrow gap between two of the wrecked cars. He stared open-mouthed, as Walsh's car was followed by two more. The driver edged slowly through the gap. The sound of glass crunching beneath the tyres could be heard despite all the other noises. Once through, the driver closed his window again and accelerated away, quickly followed by the other two.

'Nasty,' Brenda commented but just then the car's code number was called on the radio. The speed slackened only marginally as the driver picked up the handset, driving with one hand on the wheel.

'It's the Chief Constable for you, sir,' he shouted.

Walsh unbuckled his seat belt and leaned forward to reach for the phone.

'Walsh here, sir,' he said. Through the crackling the C.C.'s voice was just recognizable.

'It's all set up, Sidney. One of the Sussex cars will pick you up after Gatwick, near the Haywards Heath junction. You'll be met when you get to Brighton. I had to shout at them, they couldn't seem to appreciate the danger. I haven't been able to get through to the Home Secretary yet, though. Fortunately one of their chaps knows you. Fellow by the name of Donaldson, met you on some course or other. So you should be all right. I hope so, anyway. Good thing you sent all your mug shots on ahead, they were getting a bit stroppy about identification at one time. All right now, though. Young Finch is with me and he isn't happy. That list you gave him, those people you wanted picked up, he can only find the lab director, Holmes and Mrs Higgins, and they're kicking up a hell of a stink. We can't find the rest, at least, they aren't where they should be. I've told him to bloody well find them. We've put out calls for their cars, both here and in Brighton, thought you'd want us to do that. You all right?'

'Yes, sir, thank you. Another hour or so and we'll be there.'

'Right, you'll let me know the moment anything happens, if it does? Don't forget, I want to know.'

Walsh handed the phone back to the driver.

It was a pity Finch hadn't been able to pull in everyone on that list. If he had, there probably wouldn't be anything for him to worry about tonight. As it was, well, all the possibilities were still there, and he'd have to carry on as planned, but he ought to be a bit more sociable.

'Brenda, about your hobby, restoring china, you were

saying the other night that the paints you used changed colour, according to the temperatures they were fired at. If you don't know what shade the colour's going to end up, how can you possibly get a good match?'

He was pretty sure that he knew what she would say, but that wasn't the point; with a bit of luck he could keep the conversation going for a while, without having to do any thinking himself.

These cars, they were so quiet and so smooth it was easy to think you were in a plane, flying off to a holiday, somewhere in the sun. It wouldn't be difficult to slip into that holiday frame of mind, either, with the Gatwick turn-off signs flashing by.

Shortly after that the radio warned him of the approaching link-up with the Sussex car.

Sure enough, a white Granada took the lead.

The motorway ended and the pace dropped.

A few more questions to Brenda kept her going. What on earth had she been saying?

They were in the built-up area now, and the London road was still busy, even at this time in the morning.

Obviously they were being taken straight down to the sea front. They weren't travelling fast, but they kept moving steadily. Prinny's Palace appeared on the right; not long now. It hadn't been raining down here, funny how the weather varied from place to place. Complicated traffic light system here, with everyone changing lanes. Round the corner to the right. Was that a glimpse of the sea out there on the left? The car in front was slowing, driving the nearside wheels on to the pavement. Walsh's driver followed suit.

There it was, the Grand Hotel, on the other side of the road, a blaze of light and shiny fresh paint.

A small group was coming over to greet them. He recognized Donaldson.

A quick rub over the eyes with his fingers. Time to be wide awake, he told himself. Those characters would eat him for breakfast if he wasn't on the ball.

He opened his door, swung his legs out and went to meet them.

20

'Hello, Sidney. We met in Coventry, a couple of years ago. Remember?' Donaldson said, reaching out to shake Walsh's hand. Walsh nodded, and was introduced to the other top-ranking security staff.

He detected a faint air of condescension, or was it disbelief?

'What is this weird thing of yours that you're so afraid about, then?' he was asked by a voice that contained an element of sarcasm.

He felt hemmed in by the small group on the pavement. There was still no move towards the hotel entrance.

His mouth tightened with growing anger, and his jaw jutted forward aggressively. He saw Brenda standing with the others in a group, and motioned with his head towards the entrance steps.

'Come on,' he said, brushing through the group around him and walking up the steps into the hotel foyer.

'Here, wait a minute, you can't just bust in like this,' a voice protested behind him.

He swung round, eyes blazing angrily. 'Now, just you lot listen, and listen carefully.' He was almost snarling and baring his clenched teeth. The very fierceness of his expression brought a stunned silence to his listeners.

'One flick of a switch on this gadget,' he thundered, 'and your guards are walking about like zombies, utterly useless.

Only these,' with a wave of his arm he indicated the oddly dressed group that had followed him in, 'these, have been tested against its effects and they are the only security screen available, whether you like it or not. Now stop waffling about like a group of doddery old women. I want my lot doubled up with yours, on every access point. Like now! Where's your ground plan? Come on. Move!' He glared at the reddening faces about him.

One of the group was looking at him with clear intelligent eyes.

'Over here, sir,' he said, moving over to a corner, screened off from the rest of the foyer by blue velvet curtains.

To reach it they had to pass through the frame of a metal detector. He heard its warning bleep as he went through, and again as Brenda followed him, telling all and sundry that his group were armed as well as intruding. His anger, his emotions, were strained to such a pitch he had to fight hard to prevent himself from giggling at their consternation, but that very anger had given him the advantage, and he must maintain that.

'There are only four entrance points altogether. These two here needn't concern us. They're locked and secured until the morning. The main entrance, here, and the single rear access point, there, are double-manned, with a card-check computer link, and explosive and metal detectors. The alarms activate this control panel.'

Walsh stared at him. He wished he could remember the fellow's name. Donaldson had introduced him, and to use it now might help ease the tension.

'Roberts.'

The word was breathed into his right ear. That was Brenda's voice. Was she psychic or something?

'That's fine, Roberts, that makes life easier. Right, we'll post two over there, by the main door. You, Sergeant Masters, and you, Smith.' He nodded to the second of his two deaf ex-policemen. 'You two cover the main doors. Brenda, Joe and you two, come with us. The rest can stay here, by the control centre.' He turned back to Roberts. 'You lead the way to the back door. We'll post two of these there, then you can show me where I can get a cup of coffee.'

He'd taken a high-handed attitude, and his evident anger would be resented, particularly by the two officers who were his seniors in rank. They would never forget or forgive his having ridden roughshod over them in front of so many people. What the hell, he was right and they were wrong.

He felt a wave of lassitude flow through him as his anger ebbed away, and his legs felt tired and heavy as he strode after Roberts, down the passageway leading to the smaller, rear entrance hall.

Roberts pushed the double doors open.

'What the hell's going on here!' he exclaimed.

One of the two guards sat motionless on a chair by a computer terminal, his eyes staring blankly towards the door. The other, dressed in a dark grey suit, sprawled by the far wall, unconscious of the fact that his jacket had been pulled back from his left shoulder, exposing the empty holster beneath his armpit.

'Hell's fire!' Walsh muttered under his breath. 'It's here all right,' he said out loud, desperately trying to make his voice sound calm. 'But only a short while ago. The keys, Roberts?' Now he was almost shouting, but shouting could bring on panic. 'Roberts,' he repeated, 'the keys, the chambermaids' or the master room-keys. Where are they kept?'

Roberts looked at him blankly.

'The master keys, where are they kept? Come on, man,' Walsh asked again, shaking his sleeve.

'Downstairs,' Roberts blurted out, visibly shaken. 'In a room next to the cloakroom the chambermaids use, but we've got a man in there, guarding it.'

Walsh cast him an exasperated look.

'There's a corridor beneath this one,' Roberts added hurriedly, pointing to the door opposite. 'Stairs both ends, and a lift in the middle, but that's a service lift, we've switched it off, isolated the circuits, till the morning.'

'No time to waste. Come on, you lot,' Walsh commanded. 'You two take the far staircase. Don't forget there's a pistol against us as well now. You know your orders – don't fire unless you're forced to.'

The others were before him through the double swing doors brushing past and running down the long corridor, their feet making no sounds on the red-carpeted floor. Brenda, her brown hair swinging wildly, dived to the left, hotly followed by the nearly as agile Joe Mason.

Walsh caught a glimpse of Mason's excited face, jaw gritted and eyes aglow with the anticipation of action. A fleeting vision of a bearded man, a horned helmet and a shining sword, leaping from the high curved prow of a Viking longship with that same expression, flashed before his own wild eyes as he dashed after them, aches and pains forgotten. He was recklessly taking two stairs at a time, and going so fast that he had to bounce himself off the far wall on the half-landing, with both hands, before turning and rushing down the next short flight. He needed his elbows to fend off the double doors at the bottom as they swung back from the passage of the other two.

He found himself in a narrower corridor, long and only dimly lit compared with the one above.

Half-way down, a black-clad, hooded figure was coming out of a room on the left.

At the sound of padding of feet, the figure turned sharply, a bag appeared to fall to the floor and a black box was swiftly raised to point at the oncoming pair. Walsh steadied himself, he grasped the arm of Roberts with one hand, holding him back, and reached for the Browning

184

pistol in his inside pocket with the other. He tried to control his beating heart and laboured breathing.

Brenda was ahead of Mason, running fast, but suddenly she screamed, clasped both hands to her ears, lost her balance and fell, twisting, to the floor. The very deaf Mason leapt over her, a triumphant yell bellowing from his throat as he saw his two colleagues appear down at the far end of the corridor.

Walsh could see the figure better now. It was clearly surprised that the man was still approaching, but the box was dropped and a hand reached to its waist.

There was a sharp crack, followed by another.

Mason dived forward, his outstretched arms closed round the figure, then all Walsh could see was a pile of writhing limbs.

He ran towards them.

Brenda was back on her feet, and was there before him, grabbing the black-clad arms and twisting them high up behind the figure's back.

Mason struggled to his knees. A grimace of pain and surprise passed across his face as he looked down at the glistening drops of blood running down his right hand and dripping to the carpet.

The other two ran up, panting, to hold the struggling figure. Brenda reached for the hood, and looked up at Walsh's face.

He nodded.

'Laurelen?' he said, as the hood was dragged over the head, revealing the spitting, snarling face of the hater of order, authority and men. It was almost unrecognizable, but Walsh could just make out the once pretty features of Varney's laboratory supervisor.

Walsh shook his head sadly, and bent to pick up the black box, the cause of so much death and frustration.

'Is that it?' murmured Roberts incredulously.

Walsh pointed to the white-painted words, 'Prototype One'. 'That's it. It doesn't look much, does it?'

Brenda eased Joe Mason's jacket off his shoulders and let it drop to the floor. Mason's face was white with shock, but he stood firm with teeth clenched, determined not to allow any further expression of pain to show. Brenda ripped the shirt-sleeve open to the shoulder. There was a nasty flesh wound in the bulging muscle. Blood welled slowly from it.

'You'll live, tough guy,' she told him, with a smile.

He gave her a lopsided grin. 'You're a right little fire-raiser yourself,' he muttered.

Walsh fumbled for a handkerchief and handed it to her.

'Are you hurt anywhere else, Joe? I thought I heard two shots,' he asked.

Joe shook his head. 'No, this was the first, the second must have gone wild, I reckon.'

He winced again as Brenda pulled Walsh's handkerchief tight round the wound.

'That'll do for now,' she said.

Walsh looked round.

Roberts had retrieved the fallen pistol. 'The chap in there's just the same as the two on the back door,' he mumbled, still shocked, nodding towards the open door.

'He'll be all right. Come on, let's get back upstairs. Bring Joe's jacket, one of you.'

He turned to give Joe a helping hand along the corridor and up the stairs.

There was an animated conversation going on in the rear entrance hall. That ceased abruptly as the strange group entered.

'I've lost my gun, sir.' The suited individual looked bewildered.

'I've got the damned thing, and you won't see it again for a while,' Roberts snapped at him. 'There's a room down the corridor you can keep her in, sir, while we get sorted out, and I'll get a car to take your man to the hospital. We'd better get that arm properly seen to.'

He glanced at Walsh for confirmation.

Walsh's face looked grey and drawn. Roberts felt a twinge of sympathy. The visiting Inspector showed all the signs of having been under great strain. 'You'll probably want to use the telephone too, sir. There's one in the office down here,' Roberts said, effectively taking charge. He snapped out some more orders.

Walsh found himself ushered into a small room with a desk. He flopped down in the chair with a sigh, and picked up the phone. It took a great mental effort to remember and to dial the right number. He heard the gruff voice of the Chief Constable.

'Walsh here, sir. We've made an arrest and recovered Higgins's black box,' he said lamely, looking up as the two senior officers came in.

'The devil you have! Any problems?'

'Joe Mason's been shot in the arm. Other than that, no. No problems.'

'Well done, Sidney. If you've got the box back, there's no point in you all staying down there. Unless you want to, that is. Who the devil was it, after all that?' the C.C. asked.

'The supervisor at Varney's laboratory. I'll wait for Mason to get back from the hospital, then we'll bring Laurelen back with us.'

He heard a gruff 'Well done, Sidney' before he replaced the receiver.

Someone else started to speak, but Walsh ignored him and dialled his home number. It only had time to ring once, before he heard Gwen's anxious voice.

'It's all right, love. We've finished down here. It's all buttoned up. We'll be on our way home in a little while,' he said more cheerfully.

'Thank God for that.'

'Now I want some coffee,' Walsh said to Roberts.

It was time to make himself more agreeable to these other fellows. He could relax now, as he received their congratulations and answered their questions.

He thanked Roberts particularly, but all the time he really wanted to be on his own and to get back home. The climax had left him drained of energy; never before had he felt so tired.

A shower, a shave and a bite to eat refreshed him considerably, but it was still a great relief to him when, later, he led his team, with a morose and sullen Laurelen handcuffed to the burly Sergeant Masters, down the front steps of the hotel and back to the waiting cars.

Walsh cast a last glance up at the curtained windows of the floodlit façade above him. Their sleep should remain safe and undisturbed. He settled back into his seat as the Rover drew away from the kerb and, following the London road signs, headed rapidly north.

Brenda closed her eyes. She too was feeling very weary, and that noise from Higgins's black box had given her a headache which still persisted.

The Chief was very quiet. She wondered if he had fallen asleep. That wouldn't be so surprising after all that he'd been through. It was quite amazing, she thought, the amount of strength and the depth of resources that could be summoned by the mind from a body that ought to have been exhausted. The Chief should never really have been allowed out of hospital yesterday.

Was it only such a short time since she had sat at his bedside waiting for him to regain conciousness? It seemed so much longer than that. She had not thought very highly of the doctor for letting him go when he did, but now she could see that there might have been some wisdom behind the decision. Perhaps the doctor had sensed, in some way, that Walsh had been a man with a mission, with a purpose to fulfil, and had felt that restraint would have been the worst thing.

Not only had she seen Walsh draw on all his resources to fight his fatigue, she had also seen him as a man of action. The dramatic demonstration of the power of his personality on their arrival was a scene she would remember for a long time. She could clearly recall the amazed expressions on the faces of those senior officers. It had been quite clear to her, and to the others of the team, that the liaison with the hotel security organizers had not been very good.

Obviously they had accepted the Cambridge team as a bona fide extra force – presumably the Chief Constable had achieved that – but they had certainly failed to appreciate the danger presented by somebody armed with Higgins's machine. She rubbed her chin at the thought that, perhaps, their attitude was quite understandable. After all, the use of Higgins's machine for such a purpose had not even crossed her own mind, and she'd been on the case for days. It was another of those situations where the answer to a baffling question was so plainly obvious, when you knew the solution. Though, even now, she could not see how the threads in the case had led Walsh to the conclusions that had identified both the place and the murderer.

The car sped on.

It was no longer too dark to see the Sussex countryside. Grey shapes were visible, and the lightening sky to the east heralded the coming of the dawn.

The man beside her stirred. She could see him holding his pipe and tobacco pouch in his lap. His fingers were moving nervously, in fact the left hand was trembling.

She waited until the pipe had been lit and smoked for a while before she ventured to ask the question she had been dying to ask since she had pulled the black hood from Laurelen's head.

'Chief, just how did you work it all out? I mean, what was it that put you on to Laurelen and Brighton? I'm sure when Reg and I left your place last night you hadn't got any fixed ideas, or if you had, you certainly didn't show it,' she asked him quietly.

There was a short pause before he replied. 'It's difficult to say, Brenda. We had some people with a motive but without a clear sequence of contact and opportunity. Others had the opportunity, but a clear motive was lacking. Yes, I suppose it was all there, waiting for the last piece to fall into place. Armchair detecting in comfort, Brenda. Old-fashioned stuff,' he replied thoughtfully.

Brenda heard the click of his lighter and turned her head to look at his face, lit up by the flickering, yellow flame that was being sucked into the bowl of his pipe.

After a while he continued talking. His voice was soft and the words came slowly, almost as though he was half asleep.

'Professor Hughes talked of international terrorist organizations, but I didn't feel that we could be up against anything large, since Varney's death and that of Harrison seemed to point so clearly to someone covering their tracks. So it seemed that it must be a local person. Then came the attempt to put me out of action. That didn't make much sense, since we weren't in hot pursuit of anyone, or ready to make an arrest. But the killer couldn't be sure of that, or what our next move would be. So I came to the conclusion that in having a go at me, the killer was out to buy time. Some vitally important action was so imminent that the risk was worth taking. I thought of bank robberies and the like, but Higgins's machine solved no problems when faced with alarms and locks, only when faced with humans. But the key was Brighton, that and the ability to handle the computer data and alter the machine so quickly. Mind you, I didn't have time to chew it all over much because of the need to organize this trip, but do you remember what that

190

chap Holmes said about Laurelen? "She's a knocker-down, with nothing to put in its place," he said – even he wasn't that stupid. She was probably just as much a loner as poor Varney was, but all mixed up. A bit of a man-hater as well as a hater of organized society: dangerous mental state, that. She must have seen that with Higgins's machine, she, on her own, could strike a blow that would give her existence in this world a meaning and a purpose, as well as putting her into the history books. I've no doubts that she intended to use Varney as her accomplice originally, as much to bolster her own confidence as for the actual assistance that he might give, but she failed to appreciate his weaknesses properly. She probably dangled sex in front of him as a carrot, but wouldn't let him bite, and didn't realize the effect that that might have on him. It wouldn't surprise me at all if we find out that Varney had used Higgins's machine on her, and that romp on the bed was while she was in a state of trance and helpless to prevent it. That he raped her, I mean. That would account for him being killed in the way he was. Harrison, though – I think he might have seen something to link the two of them together. If you remember, you told him that Laurelen couldn't tell us anything about Varney's private life. Maybe when they all went to the hypnotist, something may have been said to make him think there was more going on between the two of them than they wanted anyone else to know. It doesn't matter what, she had to get rid of Harrison as well. Three murders behind her, and a daring plan to accomplish. She must have been wondering what we knew, whether there was anything that could go wrong with her plans. It would be so easy for her to convince herself that the risk of trying to put me out of action was worth the peace of mind it would give her over the next few, crucial days. Add to that her knowledge of computer programming and the shortness of the time it took to adjust Higgins's safety control, then you've got a pretty good sequence of contact and opportunity.' His voice had gradually become fainter. It was now light enough for Brenda to see that his eyes were shut and the hand holding his pipe rested, limply, on his lap.

'I'm glad it wasn't that hypnotist woman. I liked her. Felt sorry for her,' she heard Walsh say.

He was almost fast asleep, but his mind wasn't quite ready for that yet.

There had been a certain amount of luck, but wasn't that often the case? Gwen putting the television on just at the right moment, to click his thoughts into place. Maybe he would have got there anyway, without that, but probably not in time to prevent Laurelen from carrying out her plans.

He would still have to set up committal proceedings when they got back, and get Packstone working over the girl's flat. Forensic would have to provide the incontrovertible proof to tie the case up properly. It needed that. Laurelen might make a confession, but even that wasn't safe these days.

No doubt the events of the past few days would be relived, many times, in his mind over the years to come, but for now it was all over.

Perhaps he could sleep the rest of the way home.